ROSCO

THUNDER VALLEY MC

SUSAN LOWER

Time Glider
Books

ROSCO

Book two in the Thunder Valley MC Series

By Susan Lower

Published by Time Glider Books LLC

ISBN: 978-1-945274-05-3

For Charlie
And his purple garbage truck...

ROSCO

1

The music would not turn off.

Emma groaned and turned over in bed. Her arm flung out in search of her phone. With eyelids sealed shut in sleep, she fought to leave the comfort of slumber and make the music go away. It was an annoying sound, and her fingers curled around the phone. Prying one eye open, she focused on the lit-up screen—three a.m.

Not her alarm.

Who was calling at such a horrid time in the morning?

The phone stopped, but Emma was awake. She stared at the phone, gathering her thoughts when the number and the annoying music registered in her brain. Audra.

What kind of trouble had her sister gotten into now?

A sick feeling spread through her stomach, maybe from getting woken so early or maybe from the dread creeping into her soul. Audra only called when she needed something.

The call went to voicemail, and the notification popped up on the screen. Emma touched the line on her phone, and the voicemail came up. She listened and frowned.

Crying. Soft whimpering, more crying, and then a moan, as if someone was in pain.

She sat up in bed, fully awake and fully scared.

The voicemail ended, less than thirty seconds, but it was enough to send a jolt of fear and protectiveness through her brain. She called the number back, listened to it ring. "Pick up."

She chewed her lip. It didn't even go to voicemail.

Emma tried again. *Dear Lord, what kind of trouble has she gotten into?*

No answer.

Emma got up, rubbed her face as she went into the bathroom. She turned on the low light above the mirror and splashed water on her face. What should she do?

She texted, *Call me back. I'm awake now. What's wrong?*

A small part of her made her more worried while the other part of her sleep-deprived mind begged her to go back to bed. She only had three more hours to get some rest after staying up past midnight to catch up on notes for the Flanagan case and reviewing the court notes for the Mitchell custody dispute.

A few more hours would help her deal with whatever kind of meltdown Audra was having. Probably a broken heart. She'd heard Audra sobbing over guys before, the ones her father refused to let her date, and for a good reason.

It wasn't like Audra to call crying. Most of the time, like their mother, Audra needed money.

Who did she owe?

Had someone hurt her?

Emma could not settle back down in bed, knowing her sister might have gotten hurt.

She looked at her screen. No message from Audra.

It was too early to call the office.

Where are you?

No response. Emma went back in her room and got dressed, mumbling, "Lord help me, if this is a ploy to get money, I'll never speak to her again!"

Not true, but she slipped on a pair of sensible flats and grabbed her zip-up sweater. She found a pair of slacks and a blouse to change into if she ran late to get to work. Now all she needed was to find her keys and a Sheetz for coffee.

Why was she doing this?

Right, Audra was her sister. If she didn't look out for her, who would?

Not their mother, and Audra hadn't spoken to her father since she'd graduated high school two years ago.

She snatched her purse, her briefcase for work, her extra clothes, and her keys. All she needed, she prayed, was a little patience to deal with whatever mess awaited her with Audra. Oh, and lots of coffee.

———

There was never a better smell to wake up to than the strong aroma of coffee wafting up the stairs as Rosco headed down them. He rolled back his shoulders, and inside the truck garage, he found several men grabbing their joe to go.

"Ken is running late. His truck won't start. I need you to take his route with Melvin this morning," Rosco's oldest brother, Brian, said.

Rosco waited his turn, poured the last of the coffee in a mug, and put a lid on it. "Who's driving my truck?"

Melvin would complain as he always did about having to ride on the outside and load the garbage. The mornings were getting colder, and Melvin would whine that his old bones couldn't take the cold. For a man in his fifties, the guy had a lot of aches and pains.

Rosco would have to suck it up for the morning and hand over driving his regular route. It was Thursday, which meant the commercial dumpsters over on the north side were due for emptying.

"Ken can take it when he gets in," Brian said.

His brother, stouter in the middle and a few inches shorter than Rosco, held onto an organized clipboard. "We have three new dumpsters to place this morning. I'll need you to take care of those when you get back."

"Where is Lucas?"

"He's backed up with painting those new two-yarders that Kevin built last week."

Kevin, married to their sister Nicole, had been sucked into the family business.

"You ready to roll?" Melvin asked, holding a steaming cup of coffee and wearing a grin on his face as wide as the county.

Rosco scowled. "Just this once." He looked pointedly at Brian. Their father may have given each of his five kids a division of the trash company, but that didn't mean Rosco had to like his extra duties. Brian oversaw the drivers and their routes, while Rosco oversaw the trucks. Everyone in the family had a hand in keeping the company running. His sister, Nicole, coordinated the roll offs for construction use.

"Come on, kid. It looks like we're going back to college." Melvin whistled as he headed toward their truck.

Brian smirked, and Rosco refused to comment. Of course, Melvin would get cheery in the morning. He wasn't the one who had to grab an extra set of gloves and deal with outside trash at three in the morning.

Mostly, the route wasn't too bad. They hit the college commons around four thirty, and Rosco hopped down from the truck while Melvin backed towards the dumpsters behind the row of houses.

He held his breath, directing and helping Melvin for the hundredth time, hoping he wouldn't hit anything or pull up at the wrong angle.

This early in the morning, Rosco held onto the positive thought this was the worst pickup spot on the route and then they'd be home free.

He walked up to the set of dumpsters. Trash spilled over

one, and he grabbed the bags to heft them in the back of the truck when he heard a sound.

He paused. At first, it sounded like the faint whimper of an animal.

Thinking it was a cat, Rosco tugged on the bag and tossed it to the truck, but then something moved in the pile and he slid his gloves on tighter.

He had seen his fair share of things as a garbage collector and crouched down, expecting the scurry of a rat or a cat to come flying out. He pushed aside several trash bags there by the dumpster. With the lid flipped back and the dumpster overflowing, he made a mental note to have his sister Nicole call and talk the college into adding another dumpster if this was going to become the norm.

However, as he pushed another bag out of the way, Rosco's blood went cold. Fog puffed from his breath in the chill of the morning, but it cinched his gut as a piece of thick bloody cloth moved between the bags.

He reached in, careful, and tossed aside a pizza box. He hunched closer and pulled back the cloth.

A newborn baby, no bigger than his two hands put together, squirmed and whimpered. Its eyes weren't open, and Rosco picked it up, bloodied sweatshirt and all.

He heard the door of the truck and stood with the infant in his hands.

"What have you got there? I figured you needed a hand; you weren't going as fast as before." Then Melvin's eyes rounded. "Is that what I think it is?"

Rosco stared down at the baby. Red and blue, it was too small to be out here with nothing but an oversized sweatshirt wrapped around it. "Call 911."

Melvin tossed off a glove, reached in his pocket, and pulled out a phone. Thank you, God, he had it on him.

He dialed, his hands and his voice shaking. Only then did Rosco realize his own hands trembled beneath the life they held. He secured the sweatshirt, brought the child closer against his chest, and had no clue what to do as Melvin gave the dispatcher the address and called in for help.

Campus police arrived first, followed by paramedics, and until they got there, Rosco slipped into the truck with the child and turned up the heat.

Who could do this?

Such tiny little fingers. For a brief second, he almost thought he saw the baby try to open its eyes.

Melvin paced outside the truck, still on the phone with the 911 dispatcher.

Rosco handed the newborn over to a paramedic, who immediately took the infant into the back of the ambulance. In no time, sirens wailed, and the ambulance took off with the baby headed to the hospital.

Rosco stood with the campus police, a balding guy named Ed, and showed him where he found the baby.

"Probably only a few hours old," the paramedic said before taking the infant and heading to the hospital. A police officer, a woman with dark hair and skin, stayed with the paramedics before the ambulance took off. Rosco inquired which hospital as Melvin approached him.

"Some college girl got herself in trouble and didn't want anyone to know. They have places for girls like that to get help," Melvin said, with a shake of his head.

"Why don't you call Brian and tell him to send another truck to finish our route? We'll dump this after we finish here, but it'll take a while." Rosco took off his gloves, his hands cold inside anyway. He tucked them in his back pockets. He would call his brother later and explain. They didn't have any backup drivers, and knowing his brother, he'd get a truck to see the job done.

The local cops called in the campus police and he answered a string of the same questions again. All the while, in the back of his mind, a million questions of his own formed.

"We received a call. A girl is missing from the apartments," the woman cop said. "We should head and check it out. The sister is waiting there. The roommate isn't there, either."

"You'll need to leave this. You won't be able to clean up the trash until our forensic finishes," another police offer said to Ed when he motioned toward the trash.

"We'll need to investigate further and possibly dig around," the female cop said.

"I understand," Rosco said.

Did they think the mother was inside one of those dumpsters?

Rosco sent Melvin on without him. He stuck around as another team of police officers arrived and searched through the line of dumpsters.

He walked out around the corner of the houses, down a few doors. The campus police stood outside an apartment. Ed and a city cop talked with a woman standing about his height, with dark brown hair and a red sweater.

He hadn't meant to spy, and he stayed far away enough not to interfere. But then the woman looked at him, her face pale, and her eyes dull with shock and information overload. Was this the sister?

Ed cleared his throat. "He's the one who found the baby."

She nodded at him and then returned her gaze to the city cop, who asked her another question.

Rosco sat down on the steps of a nearby apartment porch and pulled out his phone. He couldn't bring himself to leave until he knew the baby and its mother were okay.

2

After discovering both her sister and her sister's roommate were not at home, Emma panicked.

She called campus police, who came after she shared the voice message with them, and another incident call came in shortly after.

Someone found a baby in the dumpster behind Audra's apartment building.

No one said the baby was Audra's or even the missing roommate's, but the two events happening at the same time couldn't be a coincidence.

"They found the roommate. She was staying overnight with her boyfriend." Emma had almost forgotten about the woman cop.

"And did she…"

"No." The lady cop shook her head. "But she confirmed seeing your sister wearing the sweatshirt when she left around seven o'clock last night. For the record, she said they don't have a close relationship. Although she mentioned her roommate was acting strangely and disappeared for a while when she first moved in last semester. Do you know anything about it?"

"Yeah, she does that. I think it comes from jumping from home to home when she was a kid, between her father and our mother." Emma rattled on, worry rushing her words. "We're sure this baby is my sister's? I mean, it's hard to hide a pregnancy, right?"

The lady cop stared at her.

"Right," Emma said slowly.

"Forensics is doing a sweep of the apartment. We'll do everything we can to find her. Don't worry."

"She probably got scared. Ran away." It would explain the crying on the phone. The three a.m. wake-up call. *Oh, Audra.* Emma's heart grew heavy, her fingers digging into the bloodied UPJ sweatshirt they asked her to identify.

Hours later, she stood in the hallway of the hospital's maternity ward. On the other side of the glass, a nurse dressed and swaddled the small infant and laid it down in an incubator. The tiny little human appeared too still, too doll-like, and it made her heart squeeze. A dozen different wires and tubes came out of the clear glass incubator attached between baby and machines.

How could Audra have done this?

Making the baby part, she could believe, but the abandon her child part—no, not abandon. Emma took a shaky breath. They'd found the little one tossed in a dumpster. Garbage. She fisted the sweatshirt, her younger sister's life blood and sweat in the material. If her sister were in the shirt, Emma might have bodily harmed her. She needed to calm down.

At least their mother had enough sense to leave them with their fathers before taking off. *Oh Lord, this is my mother's fault.* Then she shook her head. "This is my fault," she whispered. "I'm so sorry, baby."

She went to pull the sweatshirt tighter when the police officer took hold of it and tugged gently. "I'll need to take that back for evidence."

Tears prickled her eyes. Emma glanced down at the sweatshirt a moment before she released it. Not knowing what to do with her hands, she stepped closer to the glass, put her hand against it, and stared at the small being fighting to survive in the incubator. So small. So innocent.

It was Audra's sweatshirt. She gave it to her for her birthday, two sizes too big, just the way her sister liked to wear her sweatshirts.

What else had her sister been hiding from her?

"Social Services will be here soon," the lady cop said.

Emma swallowed down her emotions and nodded.

Without thinking about it, she knew she couldn't allow this child to fall into the system. *It isn't supposed to be this way, God. It's not fair.*

Life never was.

Less than a half hour later, squeaking heels came near. Flats, pleated pants, and a crocheted scarf, she'd forget what the woman approaching her wore later. "I'm Janet Summers, the caseworker assigned to our young John Doe. Are you the one who found the child?"

"No, and his name is Isaac," Emma said, keeping her voice low, controlled. The baby slept, and the nurse moved away. Only then did she turn and face the social worker.

"I'm sure the adoptive parents will take your suggested name under consideration." Janet pulled out an iPad and switched it on. "The police contacted our service. Since there is a family member present, I must ask if they have charged the mother?"

"There have been no charges pressed," Emma said.

"We have not located the birth mother," the officer said.

"I see. Do you think this is more than an abandonment case?"

"My sister is missing." Emma kept to the facts. While her sister might have run off because she was scared, finding Audra would give her time to sort out this mess. If the baby belonged to Audra, then why wouldn't she have told anyone?

Of all the things her sister had done in the past, Emma couldn't believe Audra would throw away a baby.

But she was their mother's daughter.

That chilling fact iced over her veins. Is this what her sister thought one did with babies? Throw them away? Their mother hadn't exactly wanted them, but she'd given them to their fathers. Emma took a deep breath against the closing of her lungs.

The lawyer inside her reasoned that the sweatshirt, the blood, and a DNA test would prove if Audra was the mother, but Emma had a feeling the results would only worsen her fears.

"I understand this is difficult. According to the report, the child was found in a dumpster."

Emma tightened her lips, afraid to say something that she would later regret, and which would go against Audra getting Isaac back.

"I'll have a word with the doctor, and we'll go from there," Janet said, pasting on a polite smile.

The lady officer said, "Since you're here, I'll leave this in your hands."

Emma watched the officer go. Janet smiled and moved to motion toward the nurse. Emma crossed her arms. Since the doctor hadn't checked back yet with them, she said, "He's about 30 weeks. He'll need to stay in the NICU for another two or three weeks."

"Your relationship to the child?" Janet was looking at her iPad.

"I'm his aunt." Emma felt the quiver in her voice. She took a deep breath. Not even her last breakup with a guy had unsettled her this deeply. "His mother is my sister."

"And you're sure your sister is the birth mother?" Janet asked.

Emma stared hard at the woman.

Janet held up a hand. "I have to ask. The mother is missing, and it's my job to do what is best for the child."

"I understand that." And she did. Emma gazed back at Isaac. She shouldn't have blurted out the name or even given him a name without Audra's consent, but Audra didn't get a say, not when she'd run away.

"Then should I assume because you are here that you plan to take custody of the child once they release it from the hospital?"

"Him, not it." Emma got the chilly feeling of realization and tried not to shiver. A baby at twenty-seven wasn't part of her life plan.

"Excuse me?" Janet asked.

"You called my nephew 'it' when you referred to him." It would be hard to keep her defense mechanisms from going up.

Janet tucked her iPad under her arm. "I apologize. You understand we'll have to confirm your relationship with the child, do a home inspection before we can release the child to you?"

"I am quite aware. I think you'll find I'm more than qualified to care for my nephew." Emma reached in her bag, pulled out her card, and handed it to the social worker.

"You're a lawyer?"

"I specialize in family practice." Emma glanced again at Isaac. His little face scrunched up in sleep, and she relaxed a little.

"Your name is familiar. You were on a child case a few months ago?"

"I do a lot of child custody cases."

Janet placed the card in her pocket. "Then I'm sure we'll be seeing a lot more of each other. Is a week enough for you to prepare your home for the first inspection?"

Emma calculated in her head. She needed a crib, a car

seat, and some diapers. She could do this. Couldn't she? A baby.

The doctor mentioned potential complications that could happen with premature births when she first got to the hospital. Emma wouldn't consider them at this moment, nor the possibility of this baby not leaving the hospital. He was a fighter, and if he had even half the strong will of his mother, he'd survive.

"Of course." She bit her lip, breathing through her nose.

For these are the plans I have for you.

Her smartwatch beeped, and she checked the message. Little Isaac wasn't going anywhere. He needed the incubator, and she'd only be a minute. "I have a call I have to take. I'll be right back."

She stepped out of the maternity ward to the waiting area down the hall where cell phones were allowed and stopped by the window. She called the office back, and Lori answered the phone. "Mr. Everson is here for his two o'clock. I thought you'd like to know."

Emma turned away from the glass. Spotting a guy sitting close to the vending machines, she turned back toward the window when he caught her looking in his direction. She'd seen him in front of Audra's apartment.

What did he want?

"Emma? What would you like me to do?"

"Oh. Right. What is he doing there? I told Mary Ann to reschedule all my appointments today. I have a family emergency."

"I'm not sure. I can explain to him and reschedule. I hope everything is okay," Lori said.

The guy stood up, and she watched his reflection in the window. He shoved his hands in his pockets, and Emma tried to ignore the way his hair swooped down on his forehead. He wore faded jeans and laced-up worker boots. He'd discarded his jacket on the chair next to him. Emma tore her gaze away before he caught her staring.

No man had a right to look that good after tossing garbage all morning.

"Emma?"

She squeezed her eyes closed. *Focus, Emma. Focus.*

"I'm sorry, Lori, it's been a long morning. I need to find my sister, and my nephew is in the hospital."

"You have a nephew?"

Usually, she shared very little about her life with anyone. She hardly knew Lori, but she couldn't keep it from spilling out.

"Apparently, I do. He was born this morning." She wouldn't give more details. The last thing she needed was to have her life become the next water cooler news.

"Oh, congratulations."

"I'll be back in the office tomorrow, but I need to cut my hours the next few days if you could not make any new appointments for me this week. I need to help my sister." Find her sister. *Oh, Audra, where are you?*

3

Rosco shoved his hands in his jeans pockets and rocked back on his boot heels. He waited for the woman to finish her phone call.

Under the glow of the light in the waiting room, her brown hair sparkled with red highlights. A deep line creased between her brows as she spoke. Spotting him, she smiled faintly, and turned her back. He got that she wanted privacy, so he looked down at his bootlaces and minded his own business.

The lady officer with the campus police had been kind enough to give him a ride. Both he and the female officer had the same intention to check on the baby and ensure the little guy was going to be okay.

Holding that small life in his hands, only hours ago, Rosco felt a sense of responsibility for what happened to the infant. He'd held babies before—his sisters were both mothers—and he knew this little guy shouldn't have been that tiny. It was almost impossible not to care about that small life, he discovered. A part of him wanted to protect the baby, while the other wanted to hunt down the mother. From what he gathered, the mother was in trouble, and he saw the distress on the woman the police told him was the missing mother's sister. They hadn't given him a name.

So he waited, rocking back again on his heels, a habit he developed when having to stay still.

As she got off the phone, the woman turned, pushing back a strand of her hair and tucking it behind her ear. Mesmerized by the movement, it took his brain a moment to register her soft-spoken question.

"You're the one who found my sister's baby in the trash."

"Yeah, I am. How is the baby?" he asked.

She put her phone back in her purse. "The baby is premature, so he'll need to stay in the NICU for a while. Hopefully, that will give me time to find my sister and settle things with Social Services."

She rolled back her shoulders, and Rosco could see the tension there, the dark circles under her eyes. He knew from his sisters that telling a woman she looked like she could use more rest wasn't a good idea.

"I'm glad I found him in time." The fact she said *he* hadn't slipped his attention. "This has been quite an unexpected morning. I'm Rosco Reynolds. Can I grab you a cup of coffee or anything?"

"Reynolds as in the trash company?" She tilted her head.

"Yeah, family business." His jacket parted as he shrugged, revealing his company shirt and his name *Rosco* with the company logo embroidered over the left pocket on his chest.

"Listen, I appreciate what you did this morning. Isaac could be dead right now if you hadn't found him."

"But?" He could hear it in her tone, saw it in the way her chin lifted and her face held onto her blank expression. He wouldn't want to play poker against this woman.

She put on a smile, fake, for it didn't reach her eyes. "This is a family matter. It's personal, and I need to make sure Isaac is taken care of, and I really need to find my sister."

Exhaustion filled her voice. He understood, too well, that

having been up since three in the morning could sap one's mind.

"Why don't I get us some coffee, and then we can talk and see if maybe I can help."

He wouldn't take no for an answer. No one else had arrived since he got here, and he had the feeling she was all alone. No other family called or came. The nurse who flirted with him had said as much.

"I need to get back. The social worker is here, and I need to ensure she isn't speaking with the doctor or nurses and trying to make arrangements for his care or custody without me."

"I'll grab us that coffee, and I'll be right here waiting for you."

She gave him a long look as he shifted his weight under her assessment. Not saying another word, she headed out of the waiting room, and he realized she hadn't given him her name. There was still time to finish introductions. He had no intentions of going anywhere anytime soon.

But he thought, if he had gone back with Melvin and gotten his bike or even his truck, he would have run to Starbucks, but plain hospital coffee would have to do. He grabbed extra sugars and a few creamers, thinking he should have asked her how she liked it.

Returning to the waiting room, he sat her coffee on the table. He'd never gotten that second cup back at work. At least this spared him listening to Brian complain about another inconvenience in the schedule. Brian, his older brother, offered to come and be here with him, even if he didn't understand why Rosco insisted on checking on the baby.

It wasn't every day he found a small human being wrapped up in a college sweatshirt and left in the trash. Why hadn't the woman come to the hospital to give birth and given the baby up for adoption if she didn't want it?

It wasn't his place to judge. He had no idea of this

woman's circumstances or who she was. Audra Barnhart. The campus police officer might have told him too much, but the baby's mother had a name, if that was indeed the child's mother.

Audra's sister also intrigued him. Preoccupied with the baby on her mind. Would she even remember his name? The way she looked at him made him lift his arm and sniff. Nope, couldn't have been that.

And yet, he still couldn't walk away and leave her or the baby. The moment he'd heard that precious baby whimper and pulled it from the trash, it became his business.

He'd about convinced himself to go when she returned. "Everything okay?"

She sat down at the table, took two sugars and three creamers for her coffee. "You get woken up to your sister crying in a voicemail. Find her missing and discover she had a baby and tossed it in the trash. Then, you have to cancel all your appointments for the day to figure this mess out. Everything sound okay to you?"

He bit back the smile at her sarcasm and sat across from her.

The woman had a right to express her frustration. He wrapped his hands around his coffee and watched her lift her own coffee to her lips, figuring her first sip would be lukewarm at best.

"If it makes you feel any better, I don't wake up every morning figuring I'll find a baby in the trash. I find some interesting things in my line of work, but this is a first."

She lowered her gaze to the coffee.

"I'm sorry you're going through this."

"Thanks for the coffee." She gathered her purse, as it slipped from her shoulder. "I appreciate you stopping by the hospital, but I am afraid my nephew is in God's hands now."

"What will happen to him?"

She stared down at her cup, her thumb brushing across

the lid. "That will depend on him and my sister. Once he's strong enough to leave the hospital, he'll be placed in a home or with a relative."

"With you?" Rosco asked.

She took another sip of coffee, her perfectly lined brows drawing together. "I don't know. I'm not prepared to care for a baby, but given the options I think that would be the wisest choice. I can't see Isaac placed with strangers. In the meantime, I need to find my sister and make her face the consequences of her actions."

Her voice grew a little harsh, and he detected the bitterness.

"Let's hope the cops find her before I do." She took another drink of coffee and leaned back. "I really should go. I need to check in with work again and then make some calls. The cops told me to stay here or stick to home in case she comes or calls, but if I know my sister, she's probably run off like our mother."

Rosco reached out and placed a hand over hers on the paper cup of coffee. "I think you should listen to the cops. I have a friend on the police force, and I know they'll do everything they can to find your sister."

She gave him that fake smile, a section of her hair falling forward. "You don't know my sister. She's just like our mother."

She swirled the coffee in her cup. She had the most beautiful eyes, he thought, the perfect mix of green and blue.

"I shouldn't have said that. I'm sorry. I have to go. Thank you for the coffee and thank you again. Not many people would care enough to come to the hospital and check on the baby."

She stood, and Rosco rose with her. "I'll be back to check on him again and on you. I'd like to help if you'll let me."

"Why would you want to do that?"

Several reasons ran through his head. He wanted to make

sure the baby ended up with good people. He wanted to see her smile for real. It was his Christian duty, but no, he had brothers and sisters, too. And they all seemed to do stupid things from time to time, but they were always there for each other. Something told him this woman needed someone there for her, too.

He'd gotten used to being the good friend, the brotherly sort of pal that women always wanted to hang out and rely on, but never date.

Any of those reasons and all of them wrapped together had him confessing, "Because, from the moment I picked up that baby, I got attached to his future."

He could have told her he was a nice guy and watched her walk out of the room and never give him a second glance.

She had an oval face and long brown hair any man would find attractive. She stood to where she could look him in the eye, and he held his breath, hoping she would accept his offer.

"Do you think your friend at the police force will be able to help assist in finding my sister?"

"It's worth a try."

She reached in her purse, pulled out a card, and handed it to him. "Here. This is where you can reach me."

Rosco took the card. *Emma Harris, Family Practice Attorney.* "Are you hungry, Emma? I know I am, and I can't imagine you've had breakfast, and it's after lunch now."

———

The first twenty-four hours of someone gone missing was always the most crucial time of the search. Emma left several messages for Audra and checked her phone about every hour throughout the day and the night. She prayed no matter where her sister had gone, Audra was safe.

Emma managed to reschedule her appointments at the firm so that she'd have every other morning or afternoon off to visit Isaac at the hospital and do a little searching of her own to find Audra.

She'd called everyone she could think of, including her mother. To her relief and dismay, her mother hadn't answered, and she hadn't left a message. Would Deb notice or care? By now the police would have contacted Deb, wouldn't they?

On the second day, the NICU nurses told Emma about the good-looking man who stared at Isaac through the glass. They weren't sure how he got past security, but he'd fit the description of the man who found Isaac.

The nurses' description hadn't been wrong. Rosco Reynolds was a handsome man. His boyish good looks and his very presence made her feel at ease while they drank coffee in the waiting room. He'd been so easy to talk with, and she noticed his hands.

There was something about his hands, curled around that cup, that had her thinking how comforting it would be to have them hold her. They'd held and cradled her infant nephew, holding him with such care until the ambulance arrived and the EMTs took Isaac to the hospital.

He'd saved Isaac's life. What would have happened if he wouldn't have noticed that precious baby in the trash?

Emma's heart sped at the thought.

He cared about Isaac, but she couldn't allow emotions to sway her. In her line of work, one could easily get their heart broken. The law didn't always work in favor of the heart. Besides, she had no room in her life to fantasize about relationships or a guy like Rosco Reynolds.

It wasn't even his profession that kept her from wanting to get to know him. Or she would tell herself that, because she had far too many responsibilities to fall for the handsome garbage man.

And maybe because she hoped he cared about Isaac and wanted to see him again she'd given permission for Rosco to see the baby. He would have to stay behind the glass, but she once read babies thrived from touch and Rosco had been one of the first to hold Isaac.

Not that any of them could. In a few more days, the doctor assured her she could go in and place her hand in the incubator and talk to her nephew. Verbal interaction, she'd read in that same baby article, would also help Isaac thrive.

She called her father, James Harris, not about to miss their weekly check-in call, and told him about Audra and the baby. "How could she do this? She's just like Mom!"

As always, her father's stern voice pulled her back into focus. "It's hard to say why she made that decision. You said she called you, so she tried to reach out to you first."

"If only she'd answered the phone. I called right back."

"Maybe she couldn't," her father said. "Have you spoken to your mother?"

That made Emma sit back. She was in the third-floor office, staring at all the legal books behind her desk. Her hand brushed across the spine of a few and paused.

"Emma?"

"I called."

"And?"

"She didn't answer."

"You didn't leave a message." In all the years her father had raised her, he never spoke an unkind word against her mother. They understood the type of woman Deb had become. Emma's father gave her the option to have a relationship with the woman who had abandoned her, but she had stayed away.

"Audra could have gone there, or she could have called your mother."

"I gave the police Deb's number. They would have contacted her by now."

"If she has her phone turned on," her father said. "It wouldn't hurt to visit her, or at the very least try calling her again, and this time leave a message. I know that's asking a lot, but it might help you find Audra faster and make sure she is okay."

"I'll think about it."

"I know you will, just like I know you'll do that right thing. Now tell me about the baby."

And she did. She told her father how she'd named the child Isaac and about the social worker, and that she had a few more days to get her apartment ready. Her heart jumped to her throat as she realized she hadn't even thought about what needed to be done to her place to bring Isaac home.

Purposely, she left out the part about Rosco coming to the hospital and offering to help. What did a trash guy know about babies? Maybe the guy was married? Did guys in that kind of profession wear wedding bands?

He couldn't have been older than thirty, but the thought of him married bothered her. Not that he was her type, or she'd consider going out with the guy.

She ended the call with her father promising to contact Deb, her and Audra's mother, and call him again with any updates.

Her father worked for a trucking company as a dispatcher, after years of driving a truck. That's how he'd met her mother, Deb, having picked her up at a truck stop and made the mistake of bringing her home.

Her father always said the one mistake he never made was Emma, and she loved him more for being there for her when her mother walked away.

As much as it pained her, Emma pushed back those emotions and tucked them away for another day. They wouldn't help her find her sister or do what was best for baby Isaac.

4

Rosco showed up late for the Thunder Valley Christian Motorcycle Club's monthly breakfast meeting. During three seasons of the year, they'd take a ride after their meeting and fellowship some nights at the Frosty Freeze.

Haden and his fiancée, Holly, had arrived ahead of him. Rosco took an empty seat by Haden and shook his friend's hand. "It's good you could make it."

He could tell by the tone of Haden's voice he'd gotten elected for something again because of his lateness. He couldn't help it. Picking up trash sometimes fell to him on Saturdays. He had to deliver and pick up rollbacks to commercial sites, and every hand helped in a family business.

"How's Charlie?" Rosco asked.

Across from him, several of the club's officers—Judy, Steve, and even Larry—sat with their coffee in hand.

"He's as grumpy as ever," Haden said.

"But he'll be there to roll me down the aisle this spring," Holly added.

"Roll?" Rosco asked.

"He thought he was going to put Hols here in a sidecar

but couldn't convince her. So, we talked him into another idea."

"I ordered him a motorized wheelchair," Holly said.

Since Charlie's accident, Holly's father had been in rehab healing. He wouldn't walk or ride a motorcycle again. Although many of them suspected it wasn't an accident. They believed a rival club, the Sharks, had it out for Charlie, and the authorities were working on gathering proof. Charlie always tried to help those he believed needed a second chance, and sometimes helping others cost more than time.

"What's new?" Larry leaned forward, and Rosco recognized that look.

Haden and Holly shared a grin. Down the table, several others smirked and nodded toward him.

"What did you all volunteer me for?"

Judy laughed. "We were just about to update the prayer list. Anything we can add for you?"

"Not me, but the Harris family. Emma's nephew is in the hospital, and her sister is missing."

Rosco had hoped to see Beast, one of the other brothers in their club and a close friend.

"Harris?" Holly asked.

"A woman I recently met."

"Is there anything we can do?" Judy asked, making notes.

Rosco flipped his mug, and a waitress came and poured him a cup of coffee. "Pray the baby thrives. The little guy is in the NICU." Rosco explained how he found the baby in the trash behind the campus commons for UPJ. "Emma got a call from her sister Audra, and she came to check on her. Audra is missing, and the police suspect she's the mother. They're still looking into it."

"The sister is Audra?" Holly asked, her gaze going to Haden, and stiffened.

"Yeah. You know her?" Rosco asked.

Haden shook his head, but Holly tilted her head, her eyes growing large.

"A girl named Audra helped me escape when Pike kidnapped me. Charlie was trying to help her get away from Pike. She stayed in my old room before the accident."

"That's right." Judy shook her finger. "I remember Charlie talking about that. Her name was Audra."

"Yeah, but she wasn't a Harris, and she wasn't pregnant," Haden said. "She was helping the Sharks try to sabotage the rally."

"What do you mean she wasn't pregnant?" Holly asked.

The waitress came back with bills, and Rosco realized he'd missed more than breakfast.

"She lived with Charlie and worked at the shop for a few weeks. I think I would have noticed," Haden said.

"Men are so blind." Holly shook her head.

"You think she was?" Leave it to Judy to get so concerned with everyone else's lives.

"She's a student. I saw her at the café, remember?" She looked at Haden. He scowled and took her hand in his, squeezing it gently. "I'd rather not. What happened is over. I'd rather not be reminded of what happened."

The Sharks president had kidnapped Holly and tried to keep the annual rally from happening downtown. They may have stopped the rally downtown, but the rally got located elsewhere, and Holly was safe. More than safe, as it helped Haden man up and ask Holly to marry him.

Rosco sipped his coffee, making sure Haden couldn't block his view while Holly spoke. "Audra helped me. Without her, I don't think I could have given Pike the slip. If she was pregnant, and that's her baby, we need to help her."

"I agree," Judy said.

"We don't know if it's the same Audra," Haden said.

"What does Emma's sister look like?" Holly asked.

Rosco motioned to the waitress for a coffee refill and

ordered a plate of hotcakes. Once the waitress went off with his order, he said, "I don't know."

"You need to find out," Judy huffed. Steve bumped her, and she sighed. "I know, stick to my prayers."

"I think praying is the best thing we can do for now. I'll have to check with Emma to see what her sister looks like. I know she's a college student. Her roommate wasn't home, and they thought maybe the baby was the roommate's, but then they found the roommate, and she was with her boyfriend for the night."

"That could just be a cover-up," Larry chimed in.

"I'm sure the police will follow up and make sure," Haden said.

"What will happen to the baby?" Holly asked,

"Social Services was there, and Emma said she'd take him rather than him go to strangers."

"It's not always safe to assume." Steve leaned back to get his wallet and pay his bill.

"She's family," Rosco said.

"Is she married? Taking on the responsibilities of a baby is a big deal," Judy said. "Sometimes Social Services makes their determination not of family, but what is best for the baby."

Rosco cupped the back of his neck. He worried about Isaac. Emma's card said she was a family lawyer. She would have the knowledge of the law behind her. He hoped. "I didn't ask, but I didn't see her have a ring on, either."

The waitress returned with his order.

All day he had been on autopilot. Thoughts of Emma and Isaac weighed heavily on his heart and his mind. He kept her card in his pocket. Having stopped by the hospital to see the baby, he also had hoped he would see her again. He debated calling her. What would he say?

"It's never safe to assume these days," Judy said.

"You should go see Emma." Holly took her purse and stood. "Find out what Audra looks like. If it's the same girl,

she had a blue streak in her hair when I saw her. I'll be back."
Holly excused herself from the table.

Haden watched her go. "She's built a little on the heavy
side, would come to about your shoulder. Nineteen, maybe
twenty now, with dark hair, and as Holly said, she's got it dyed
blue. Kool-Aid job. She was taking classes at UPJ. I don't
know what major. But if it's the same Audra, then you need to
warn the sister. Audra is with Pike, and that's not good. She
risked a lot to help Holly, so I feel we owe it to help if it is her,
and if she is the mother, then that means——"

"Pike's the father." Rosco stared down at his breakfast, no
longer hungry.

Steve and Larry rose from their chairs while a few others
lingered and talked. Judy promised to send out the prayer list
to everyone, and she and Holly said a few words in passing as
Holly returned.

"You haven't seen Beast around, have you?" Rosco asked
Haden.

"I haven't."

"Any idea how to get a hold of him?" Rosco asked.

"No, man. He's incognito, and that's all I know."

Rosco nodded.

Haden rose and patted him on the shoulder. "We'll be
outside waiting for you to finish your breakfast, road captain."

Rosco paused mid-reach for the syrup. "Road captain? So
you stepped up as vice?"

Haden grinned and shrugged. "You rode your motorcycle,
right?"

The shock must have been evident on his face, for Haden
said, "Don't worry. I've got you covered for today."

Rosco's mother had taught him not to waste food, and he
would have to pay for it. He shoved the pancakes into his
mouth and grumbled.

After the ride, he'd stop by the hospital and prayed he ran
into Emma again.

_____

No messages. No missed calls.

Besides the fact it was Wednesday, Emma couldn't concentrate on the pile of files she'd brought home to review. There were too many kids in homes that deserved better and too many parents who couldn't see the blessings they had. It was how she always felt about the torn families, the kids living in broken homes and hiding the abuse, afraid they were the ones in trouble.

The last file had made her sick to her stomach, and as she tried to pray over each one, asking God to guide her with the knowledge of the law to help protect these kids, her mind would drift to the helpless baby in the NICU. Not any baby, Isaac, her nephew.

The police were still working on proving whether Audra was the baby's mother. Anyone could have a college sweatshirt. It proved nothing. And Audra missing? Her roommate reported that Audra often disappeared for days or even weeks at a time. Did she ever show up at class?

It wouldn't take long for the hospital to extract DNA from the blood on the sweatshirt and pull Audra's health files to find a match with the baby.

Emma had a two-bedroom apartment. She used the second room as an office. After spending most of her morning packing things up, figuring out how to move her desk into her bedroom or in the living room, she stared at the empty room.

She had no clue what to do next, so she went to the hospital.

Someone had to show up and be there for Isaac. They offered her a gown and an invitation to go inside the NICU for the first time.

The little sock cap on his head and his tiny body all curled up in his incubator made Emma's chest tighten and burn. Did Audra have any idea how precious this life was before her?

They gave her a chair, and a nurse opened a little round window at the side of the incubator. "It's alright. Contact is good for them."

"He's doing better?" she asked.

"As expected. Talk to him. Touch his small fingers. It's okay." The nurse checked on another baby and its family. Both the parents—a man and a woman—sat beside each other, their hands around their child. She could hear the woman humming a lullaby, and it nearly undid Emma.

This wasn't her child, but he deserved someone to love him, but Emma wasn't sure that could ever be her.

"Hey there, buddy. I am not good at this. I know little about babies, but I know we'll figure this out. I'll make sure you're safe, and you'll be in a suitable home with people who will care for you and love you."

Conflicted, she took a deep breath. Maybe Isaac would be better off with a family. There were plenty of couples out there wishing to adopt. She wouldn't want the little guy to fall into foster care and get hustled from home to home. She saw it too many times, and it broke her heart. Without Audra's permission, though, a couple couldn't adopt the baby as their own.

She'd given up certain rights when she abandoned him. *I'll never leave you nor forsake you,* the piece of Scripture from Hebrews, had been in her mind often lately.

Tiny fingers curled around her large one, and Emma sucked in her breath. "You keep holding on, baby. Auntie Emma is here."

A small tube ran up into the baby's nose. They'd placed an oxygen clip on his little foot, and heart monitor wires poked out of the incubator. It seemed like a few seconds before the nurse came, and Emma had to withdraw her hand from him. "His lungs aren't fully developed. He needs a little help yet to breathe on his own."

She sat beside him, not knowing what to say. She couldn't

hum or sing any tunes because her father always just read to her. So, she told him the turtle and the rabbit's story and how by taking his time and setting his pace, the turtle had come out ahead of the rabbit.

As she finished the story, talking low not to disturb the other family, she looked up and found Rosco Reynolds standing on the other side of the glass. He appeared different than she'd last seen him. A vest with patches on the front covered his chest, and he watched with eyes set deep with concern. It tickled her insides, and she couldn't admit it made her happy to see him.

It was too bad they hadn't met under better circumstances. Too bad, still, Emma had no intentions to get involved with anyone. She couldn't afford the distractions of getting into a relationship. Her mother had left her, leaving her father, and it had changed him. She would never become like her mother—like her younger sister. She and Rosco could never be more than friends.

It set an ache in her, a low-grade throb that would be hard to forget.

Rosco appeared the opposite of what she imagined a guy would look like if she ever dated. She pictured the suit-and-tie type, corporate and hardworking as her father. The vest and the blue jeans gave him a rough edge that made her feel nervous. But the dimple in his chin when he grinned at her made her insides wobble.

Emma promised Isaac she'd see him again soon and went to shed the hospital gown. Out in the hall, Rosco stuffed his hands in his pockets. He leaned against the glass, looking in at her nephew.

From experience with clients, she knew he fit the stereotype of men who lacked the ability to commit. No tattoos, just steel-toed black boots and confidence radiating from him that set her nerves to flutter all over again.

"You know you don't need to keep coming back."

"I told you I wanted to help. I hoped you might be here," he said.

"The police are still looking for my sister. I don't think there is much else to do. They told me to stay home and keep my phone on me if she tries to call again. I've left her several texts and messages, but she doesn't respond. It's been over twenty-four hours now." Emotions crept up in her voice.

"Hey." He laid a hand on her shoulder. "You're not giving up, are you?"

Her vision got blurred, and she tried to blink away the moisture. She swiped at her eyes. She hadn't put on makeup this morning. It never occurred to her that she would see anyone today of importance.

He'd seen her once before, worse than this, and she tried to pull herself together. Places reversed, she doubted Audra would become a blabbering fool.

God, she just wanted to know her sister was alright. She was mad at her, yes. But she was still her only sister.

"I am not oblivious to how this works. The longer Audra is missing, the more likely we won't find her."

"The police aren't going to look as hard as we are. They don't know her as well as you do."

He kept his hand on her shoulder. The firm pressure of his touch comforted her. "As I told the police, I don't know my sister that well. We're almost a decade apart in age, and we don't share the same fathers. Audra's like my mother. She only comes around when she wants something."

Her words appeared to have drawn out sympathy from his eyes. Dark maple irises with flecks of gold swirled in his gaze, and she looked away to check on Isaac.

"She called you once."

"Probably because she was in trouble and wanted me to help get her out of it." *Oh Audra, why couldn't you have picked up the phone that first call back?*

"Then she'll call again if she can. But in the meantime, I need to ask you something."

"Why does finding my sister matter to you?" she asked.

His hand dropped away, and he rocked back on his heels, something she noticed he often did from their previous meeting.

"Because it's important to you," he said, looking sheepish.

She'd heard a lot of lines throughout the years, never one like this. It almost made her laugh. It would have been a good one, too, if she had a mind to date him.

"And," he went on, "I think I might know your sister. Or at least a brother of mine in the Thunder Valley Motorcycle Club knows a girl named Audra. I just need to know what she looks like to confirm it."

"Thunder Valley M That's why you've got the vest and the patch. That was enough reason for her not to consider dating him.

"Not the kind you're thinking. Thunder Valley is a Christian motorcycle club, and our mission is to spread the love of Christ," he said.

Be that as it may, Emma pushed aside any further thoughts of seeing him as nothing more than a means to find her sister.

5

"So, helping me find my sister is sort of like a mission to you and your cause? If you're looking to bring Audra to Christ, good luck with that." She spoke with sober certainty.

"How about we look at some photos of your sister and go from there?"

He recognized the doubt in her eyes. He got that look a lot. She either didn't believe him or couldn't figure out what he was selling. Too bad for her he wasn't selling anything. He was the only guy who drove a garbage truck by day and a motorcycle by night.

"I think I should have a picture of Audra on my phone. Maybe one from when she moved in on campus a few months ago. I can't believe she was pregnant and didn't tell me." She scrolled through her picture feed on her phone. "As I told the officer, I don't have many photos. Our birth mother might have more, but that's if you can get a hold of her. Here. This one."

She turned her phone and held it out to him. "That's Audra. It's hard to see from this angle, but she's got this blue streak in her hair."

A girl in her late teens scowled at him from the photo. She

had a round face and dark hair. As Emma said, a blue chunk of hair slipped over the girl's forehead and covered one of her eyes.

He recognized her. She'd worked for Charlie for a bit, and he'd seen her there when he visited his buddy, Haden. He pushed back his hair from his forehead and nodded. "I know her."

Emma's eyes rounded. "You know my sister? Are you sure?"

He couldn't blame her for not believing him.

Rosco shrugged. "Small world."

Even smaller coincidence.

"How do you know Audra?"

"I don't." He gave her the truth. "She stayed at a buddy of mine's place for a while. Something about having trouble with her old man. Charlie, the old president of our club, tried to help her. He gave her a place to stay and a job."

"She had a job, cleaning after hours at some club."

Anger and defeat sounded in her voice.

"You mean the Sharks' clubhouse? It's a rundown truck garage in the old part of town. I doubt Pike was paying her."

"Pike?" Emma gave him a look of confusion.

She knew little about her sister. Rosco hated to be the one to tell her.

"Pike is her old man."

"Audra's father's name is Clay. I've never heard anyone speak of him and call him Pike." She tucked her phone away.

"I see I'm going to have to teach you some biker lingo. An 'old man' isn't daddy talk. It means Pike is her boyfriend. Or at least he has a claim on her."

After the way she'd looked at his patch, he had gotten worried she wouldn't trust him.

"I see." She moved a few paces away from him. "My sister never mentioned having a boyfriend. Although, we don't talk much."

It pained her. Her face scrunched up, and Rosco resisted pulling her into his arms. *Lord, give this woman comfort where I cannot.*

The last thing he figured the family lawyer would appreciate was getting pulled into a stranger's arms. Not that he'd call them strangers anymore. From the moment he held that infant in his arms, and he met her, he knew he was where he belonged.

"Did you talk to her roommate?"

She shook her head. "I've been meaning to do that, but I've been swamped at work. I have a meeting I need to get to, but I will afterwards. Maybe this Pike guy knows something about my sister's disappearance. You said he's at an old truck garage?"

"You're not going there alone. We should start with the roommate."

"We?"

"I'm coming with you," he said.

"That's kind, but you've done enough. I should call the detective and tell him about the motorcycle gang, but first, I need to make sure."

"Which is why I'm coming with you. If Pike and his club are involved, you shouldn't go places alone. I'll call the police on my part and tell them what I know, and I'll meet you after your meeting. Just give me an address and a time."

Reluctantly, she agreed. She gave Rosco the address of her building and told him to meet her at five o'clock.

In the meantime, Rosco called his brother, Beast, and the call went straight to voicemail. He called Haden and updated him on the situation with Audra.

In the background, he heard Holly launch into a plan to help Emma prepare for baby Isaac's going-home party. There wasn't a doubt in any of their minds the little guy would pull through and thrive for Emma to take him home in several weeks.

He hoped for the baby's sake there wasn't more to this than there seemed. If Pike was the father, there was no telling what trouble would arise.

First thing, though, they needed to find out what happened to Audra and why baby Isaac was left in the trash outside Audra's campus housing complex.

Rosco went back to work for a few hours. He ran into his sister Nicole. Caden sat in her office in one of the plush chairs with an iPad in his hands and earbuds plugged in his ears. His feet swung over the arm as his head lay cradled in the back of the chair. The kid's eyes were glued to the screen as the tablet rocked side to side with him playing the game.

"The school called, and I had to pick him up early," Nicole explained.

"Shouldn't you be at home with him then?" Rosco leaned against the door frame of her office.

"He tossed his cookies at lunch. He's been fine since." Nicole spread out another set of papers. "Dan won't be home until three. What are you doing here? I thought you were scouting out a new area for service after you got done with your route this morning."

"Who told you I was out scouting?" Rosco nudged Caden. The little boy glanced at him, a chin tilt to acknowledge him, then back to his game.

"Brian did. Why? Did you not go?" She paused from looking at an invoice. "Okay. What did I miss?"

Rosco sat on the edge of her desk. He waited to see if she'd yell, but she gave him that 'spill it' look. The kind their mother gave them when they got in trouble. Even Caden glanced at him again.

"I went to the hospital to check on the baby, and the sister was there."

"You *were* scouting, just not that kind of scouting." Nicole leaned back. He had his sister's full attention. She had her hair pulled back and tied up in a messy bun. Her glasses perched at the top of her head while she did data entry work.

Like their mother, her hair was dark, as were her eyes. They filled with concern where their brother's would sharpen and accuse him of things. Nicole crossed her arms. "You like her?"

"She's a lawyer," Rosco explained.

"She'll keep you on the straight and narrow. At least that will be a relief to us from having to keep an eye on you all the time."

"I don't need you all watching over me." He got up, and Nicole frowned.

"Chill, baby brother. I didn't mean it that way."

He'd gotten in his fair share of trouble, and he'd learned his lessons along the way. His father often said some men were more hard-headed than others, but Rosco had gotten the toughest skull of all. Thank Jesus he had, or he wouldn't have gotten out of the scrapes over the years.

Unlike his siblings, he wasn't a saint, and he knew it. For the past five years, he'd managed to stay out of trouble. His father had entrusted him with the security of the offices and running his trash route. That was saying something coming from John Reynolds.

"She needs help, Nicole. You don't know what it was like finding that baby. It's a miracle the infant is alive."

Her voice softened. "I know." She looked at Caden, then back at him. "I had Marcy add him to the prayer list at church, and someone asked if there was anything else anyone could do to help. Does she need anything? I think I have some boys' things tucked under the stairs."

"I'll give you Haden's fiancée Holly's number. She and the other members of the club were thinking of doing something. I know the sister doesn't have anything for the baby." At least that had been his impression. "There is a social worker she mentioned going to do a home visit. In the meantime, they're still looking for the sister."

"It's been a couple of days now, and they haven't found her?" Nicole kept her voice low. "It's a shame. I'll never understand why things like this happen."

"I have this gut feeling there is more to this than we can see," Rosco said.

He couldn't shake that feeling. It twisted in his gut all morning while he was with Emma. He thought of how she'd looked at him, pain and maybe a bit of embarrassment for not having a better photo of her sister.

He got the idea there wasn't much love in the family, and she talked of their mother in a detached manner.

"You're doing the right thing," Nicole said, pulling down her glasses. The thin, red-rimmed, rectangle-shaped glasses made her look years older than eight years his senior.

"Thanks. I guess I should scout that new route. I told Emma I'd meet her at five."

Nicole picked up her pen, not saying a word, but it made him grin.

"Emma," he heard her mutter as he walked out the door. He liked the sound of her name, too.

6

Inside a room at the safe house, Sebastian found the young woman lying on the bed. She had on fresh clothes, a pair of sweatpants, and a long sleeve T-shirt. The heat was turned up in the room, and she had a thin blanket wrapped around her body like a cocoon.

"I brought you some food, and I've got some new bandages for when you're ready."

He set the bag down on the table. The room comprised a table with two chairs, a bathroom, a bed, and a small counter with a sink and a microwave.

Sebastian pulled out the package of gauze and bandages. He had a bottle of peroxide and a new tube of bacitracin. The other bag he put in the bathroom. The midwife he contacted had given him a list of supplies a woman might need in the days and weeks after having a baby to help with the recovery.

He walked over to the bed. A chunk of blue hair slipped over her face, and he eased down beside her. Reaching across, he pulled back her hair. Her eyes closed, relaxed. He brushed his fingers across her cheek and to her neck. Relief flooded him, feeling the pulse, slow and steady.

He moved his hand to her shoulder and gave her a gentle shake. "I can't stay long. I brought you some things. I need to look at your injuries again before I go."

She moaned, her eyes fluttering open. Glazed in pain and rimmed with dark circles, she startled. He squeezed her shoulder again, not too hard. He'd lost count of the black and blue marks along this side of her body. "You're safe, Blue."

Those idiot Sharks called her Dory, but he wouldn't remind her of what she'd been through. He knew her name was Audra, and it didn't settle any better with him for the position he'd got himself into by helping her.

Her lips parted. Her color was still too pale for healthy. She rolled toward him and stared. Those critical blue eyes were assessing him. *I wouldn't trust me either*, he thought, and he couldn't tell her who or what he was.

To her, he probably looked like a saint. Even without the badge; he kept it hidden. He was far from being an angel or a saint or anything close.

He had years of infractions to make up for, and even then, he wondered if it would be enough. He moved out of her way as she tried to stretch.

He saw the wince coming and helped her sit up. She shied back from him, and he kept his hands where she could see them.

"Hungry? I brought a couple of pints of soup, some crackers, and if you're feeling better later, I grabbed some cream horns from the bakery aisle."

"Why are you helping me?" she whispered.

Sebastian grabbed a cup and filled it with water from the bathroom sink. He handed it to her. "Let's just say you helped a friend of mine, so I'm returning the favor."

He noticed she hadn't moved the Bible from the side of the bed, where he pulled it out of the drawer for her.

"He'll kill you." She sipped at the water, and he handed her a tissue. The waterworks came every time she woke, turned on by both emotional and physical trauma. "If he finds me, he'll—"

A sob rose from her throat so that she couldn't talk.

He went to get the soup. It should have stayed hot for the ride, and the rest he put in the small fridge below the counter-top. He brought her a spoon. "Think you can eat? You need to give your body some fuel so you can heal."

"I'm not h-hungry." She slipped back down into the bed.

"I can't leave until you eat, and we look at those ribs again. You don't want me to be late, do you?" He would use whatever he needed to get her to eat and help her get better. She'd refused to go to the hospital. He'd found her in a gas station restroom, half beaten to death and hiding under a leaky faucet.

She'd called him.

He owed her, and he wanted to make sure nothing happened to her. She'd stuck her neck out, helping Holly escape when Pike had kidnapped her. She'd taken the heat and lied about Holly needing a restroom and getting past her.

Pike had been angry. He'd beaten two of the prospects and threatened to skin and flay Sebastian alive. He had plans to scare Charlie, but not enough proof of any violent attempt.

He could have arrested him then, taken him in on kidnapping charges, but the DA's office wanted more meat to bring to the grill.

He blew on the soup and handed it to Audra. Her cheek had turned green and yellow from the previous day's evidence of her bruises.

"You called no one? No one can know you're here. It's important to keep you safe."

She shook her head, a tear slipping down her face. "I am in so much trouble. They'll lock me away forever."

"Eat your soup. Let me worry about keeping you safe for a while."

He called to check in with his chief and wait for his next

orders. They'd found Audra's baby, and they assigned a new detective to the case. He reported what he knew, which wasn't much, and he couldn't tell Audra who he was without blowing his cover. As far as Blue knew, the others called him Beast, and he'd joined the Sharks months ago after abandoning his old club at Thunder Valley.

The less she knew of him, the better.

He needed to keep her safe, and he needed more time to gather information and proof on Pike. In the meantime, he couldn't let anything happen to her.

He paced while she ate. It helped him think.

"Can you tell my sister I'm alive? She's probably worried. The police are probably looking for me." She played with her soup, and he sat on the edge of the bed. He tossed his leather jacket aside.

"Just your sister?" Even that could be a bad idea.

"She's the only one who might care. I called her."

"When?" Panic was quick to stab him.

"When… after…"

"Before you called me?"

She nodded, pressing back a new flood of tears with her palm.

"Anyone else?" He needed to know.

She stared down at her soup. "My mother is upset because I haven't given her money in a while. Emma said she'd handle it. She's worthless anyway."

"Emma is your sister?"

"Yeah. Her name is Harris, Emma Harris. She works at a law firm downtown." Finally, she took a bite of the soup. Vegetable, and he kept the pint of chicken and bone broth for later.

"I'll see what I can do, but you have to promise not to contact anyone. Don't leave here without me."

Her face paled. "He knows I'm not dead."

"I don't know. There's church this evening. I'm curious about what he says."

She nodded, satisfied for now. She never said what went down before she called him. He had a good idea on his own.

"You won't tell him." It was more a plea for reassurance than anything.

"I said I wouldn't. We'd both be dead."

She took a bite and tried to put the bowl aside.

"Two more bites, then we'll look at those injuries. I'll try to bring you another set of fresh clothes tomorrow. Don't shower without me here."

He would have to figure that one out if she slipped and fell. Maybe she could shower with some of her clothes on, or just a sponge bath as he'd done the first night when trying to assess her injuries.

There had been too much blood on her clothes, and she'd confessed she'd lost her baby. "It was too early," she'd said, and his heart ripped from his chest to hear her sobs.

He shouldn't get attached. They all had heart-wrenching stories and many times would never confess they were in the wrong.

Audra had admitted her failures, her fears, and he'd respected the young woman for her honesty. He wished someone had been there when his sister had gotten backed into a corner where she couldn't escape.

For now, he'd call her 'Blue,' but soon they'd have to change her name and move her somewhere safer. "When I come back again, I'll grab some hair color. We can't have him recognizing you."

By then, he'd have a way to get her to a clinic to have her checked out properly. Chief Razek would have enough time to find another place for her until this all went down. Chances stood in her favor to have the charges of child abandonment dropped.

For now, he had to keep her alive, safe, and the child a secret to keep her from trying to do anything stupid.

She reminded him too much of Samantha. He cleared his throat, got up, and paced again. He pushed the thoughts of his dead sister in the back of his mind again.

"What's going to happen to me?"

If only he knew he could tell her. It was out of his hands, and all he could do was pray God led them through this situation in a way that kept them both alive.

———

At a quarter to five, Emma received a call for a Ross Reynolds to see her. She couldn't remember Rosco's name and assumed that Rosco was a road name since he was a biker.

He'd kept on the vest with the patch, but he'd changed to a long-sleeve shirt and dark blue jeans. He must have run his hands through his hair several times, as it went every which way. It gave him a boyish look that made him even more attractive than she cared to admit.

Rosco waited like a gentleman while she closed up her computer. She had fifteen minutes on the clock, but she wouldn't get any work done with Rosco standing in her work area.

"I'm early, so if you need to finish anything up, don't rush on my account."

Her heart had taken on the beating of a hummingbird wing. She packed several files in her bag to take home. "It'll take me most of the night to get through the rest of these. Taking work home is part of the job."

She pressed her tongue to her cheek. She hardly knew the man, and she was explaining her life to him.

"Anything I can do to help?" he asked. The deep timbre of his voice had a calming effect on her.

No one had to tell Emma she took on too much, but she

had to prove her worth in the firm. She wanted people to know she was the best and she could get the job done.

She looked down at the files in her bag and wondered how she would juggle her case kids along with Isaac. A heavy weight settled on her chest, and she found it hard to breathe. What if the police never found her sister? What then?

She'd never had much of a mother. A mother that read stories and tucked her in. Sure, her father dated, but he never committed again after her mother had run out on them. What if she failed at caring for others?

"You've done more than enough," she tried to assure him, grabbing hold of her desk for stability.

Rosco frowned, his gaze going over her face, and he stepped forward.

"Hey there," he whispered. "It's going to be okay."

It was all she needed for the flow of tears to come forth. She gulped for air like a drowning woman and swiped them away so they couldn't drown her. He pulled her against him, and her body racked with sobs. She'd held them in all this time. He ran his hand down over her hair. His other hand secured around her shoulders, and she pressed her hands against his solid chest. Warmth surrounded her, and he spoke gentle, encouraging words as she cried.

It had been a long time since she'd allowed anyone to hold her this close or let them see past the invisible shield she tried to keep around her. Emma pulled back, placed her hand on the damp place on his shirt. 'I'm sorry. I don't know what came over me."

He rubbed her arms. "I do. You've been keeping it all in, haven't you? Do you want to sit down before we go?"

She heard someone walk down the hall and glimpsed them going past the doorway. He'd left the door open. Both relief and dread filtered through her. Who had seen her let her guard down? How long before it got around the office that she couldn't keep her emotions intact?

"I think it would be better if we go."

"I'll drive."

She laughed, more to relieve the nervousness building up inside her. She turned away and gathered her things. "I'm not sure I'm dressed for getting on the back of your motorcycle."

"I brought my truck. You'd be warmer inside the cab than if you were on the back of my Harley. Although," he made a face deep in thought, then said, "maybe another time."

She blushed, scarlet heat rising up her neck, and she ducked for him not to notice.

"I parked my car in the parking garage. You can follow me."

Rosco took her by the elbow, turned her to look at him. "Breathe, Emma. I'm going to drive, and you're going to ride with me. You need to fix your makeup, and I can get us there safely. We're going to talk to your sister's roommate. Together."

Emma wasn't sure why she felt so anxious about getting in the truck with Rosco. She knew he wouldn't hurt her, but in the back of her mind, a dozen scenarios played out. She fixed her makeup using the mirror on the visor. What was in it for Rosco if they found her sister? He knew her sister, or at least he said he *knew of* her. He'd been the one to find the baby, but what vested interest did he have in helping her?

She'd learned a long time ago, with Deb, that everyone had an ulterior motive. Emma hoped, for all their sakes, she was wrong this time. It hadn't escaped her thoughts that Rosco could have known her sister more than he let on. For now, she would trust the facts, and the facts were Rosco wanted to help.

7

A little after six, Emma knocked on Audra's apartment door. Rosco stood beside her, giving her a hopeful look. Inside, music blared, and he rapped on the door louder in case her knock hadn't been heard. The door yanked open, and a young woman around the age of twenty glared at her. Her blonde-streaked hair was pulled back in a ponytail, and she held onto the door. First, the young woman's eyes drifted to Rosco and his motorcycle club vest. She leaned into the door. "Listen, I already told the last guy that was here that she's not here, and I don't know when she's coming back."

Emma shifted her gaze to Rosco.

"Yeah, so—" The young woman tried to close the door.

Rosco's hand pressed against the door, stopping her. "What man? What did he look like?"

Her eyebrow shot up. "Are you the police? Because I'm tired of you all coming around here. I've got studies to do, and you all are freaking me out."

"Hey, babe, who's there?" a male voice shouted from behind her.

Emma's adrenaline kicked up a notch. Afraid the girl

would shut them out, she said, "I'm Emma. Audra is my sister, and this is Rosco. Are you Cassy?"

Behind Cassy, a lanky guy stood. He looked like he could play on the basketball team, and he gazed out over Cassy's head at them. "What you want? She's already told the police what she knows. Leave her be."

Rosco stiffened beside her. She stepped closer, even though she wanted to step back. "Audra is my sister. May I come in? I won't be long."

Cassy glanced up at the guy.

"Sure, but not him. You tell your friends to stay away from Cassy. They have no right to threaten her."

"If they threatened her, they're no friends of mine," Rosco said.

"Yeah, well, they wore a vest just like you," he said.

Rosco tapped his patch, a cross with a banner. "Did the patch look like this one?"

Cassy frowned and shook her head.

All the while, Emma tried to remain calm and said a brief prayer for Cassy to feel comfortable enough to let them inside.

"What did it look like?" Emma asked, the cross-examiner in her kicking in.

The door opened a little, and the guy shrugged. Cassy stepped back, an invitation to come in, but Emma and Rosco stayed on the stoop of the porch. She wouldn't force her way in or make them feel uncomfortable in her sister's apartment. Someone else had come asking questions. Were they looking for Audra, too?

Uncertainty registered in Cassy's eyes. "A fish. Maybe a shark."

Rosco's arm had gone around Emma's back, and she felt his hand ball into a fist. His jaw had tensed.

"Do you know them?" Cassy asked.

"Sharks. You're right to be cautious. Was it a big guy with a beard?"

Cassy's boyfriend draped an arm around her shoulders as they backed up a little more.

"Can I come in?" Emma asked.

Cassy nodded, and they stepped inside far enough to shut the door and lock the cold outside. The days had gone from chilly mornings to warm afternoons to nippy nights for early October.

"No. I've seen that guy. He picked up Audra a few times on his motorcycle."

"Did she tell you who he was? His name?" Emma asked.

"Audra doesn't say much. We don't talk. Like I told the police, she comes and goes as she pleases. Sometimes I don't see her for weeks. I think she stays with him or somewhere else."

Audra's roommate knew more about her sister than Emma did. Why hadn't she taken more time to get to know her sister all these years? Why had she let her bitterness toward Deb and their situation keep her from being around more?

Rosco's hand moved up to her shoulder, gave her a gentle squeeze.

"Did Audra ever mention being afraid? Or any trouble she might have been in?"

Cassy shook her head again. The boyfriend found his spot back on the couch. There were two college algebra books open on the coffee table, a laptop, and a couple of paper notebooks lay spread apart.

"Did you know my sister was pregnant?" Emma asked, almost afraid to hear the answer. She should have known. Audra should have felt comfortable enough to come to her, and she hadn't. Had she gone to Deb? She doubted Audra would have gone to her father, Clayton Barnhart, not with him in jail for dealing drugs last summer.

Was it Deb or Clay who had gotten Audra involved with the biker gang, or had she done it all on her own?

She'd promised her father she'd speak to Deb, and Emma had been putting it off like a dentist appointment. Inwardly, she cringed.

"She asked me for money a couple of weeks back. I figured it wasn't for rent because we pay for the semester. Then she disappeared for a few weeks, and then when she came back, she said someone named Charlie was going to help her take care of it. That's all I know."

"Did you tell that to the police?" Rosco asked.

"No." Cassy frowned. "I didn't think that was important. Audra asked for money from time to time. I guess her parents don't help her much to go to school, and I know she works a couple of jobs to pay to make her way. So, when she's never here, I figured she was working or hanging out with the motorcycle dude. Although, he looked like he was old enough to be her father, so maybe he was?" She lifted her shoulders and her gaze to look at Emma.

"No. It wouldn't have been him. You said others came around?"

"Yeah, the ones with the Jaws patch. He was about average height with long, black, greasy hair. He had a tattoo on his neck, and the guy with him had a scar across his nose. I'm wondering if Audra owed them money."

Emma's stomach sank. What had her sister gotten into? Like mother, like daughter? It made her nauseous to think about.

"Listen, I don't want any trouble. I'm trying to go to school to be a nurse, and Jared and I want to get married after graduating next semester. I don't need this." Cassy's voice turned to a whine.

"I understand." Emma understood all too well. Like Cassy, she never wanted to get involved in the things that would cause her reputation any dings or take her from her comfort zone. It wasn't her problem. It wasn't her business, until it was.

Audra had made it her business when she'd tossed away little Isaac.

"Do you mind if I go into my sister's room? I won't take long, and then we'll leave."

"Sure," Cassy said. "The police already searched it. You can take what you want or box it all up, whatever."

Emma led the way. She'd been here once when she helped Audra move in. Her little sister hadn't had very much, just her clothes and a beloved furry blanket. The apartments came furnished, and Emma helped Audra buy a used laptop at the beginning of school. Through financial aid and loans, she had enough to buy books and ensure Audra got a meal card and a place to stay in addition to covering her tuition.

The room was small, with a twin-size bed, a desk, and a dresser. The mirror on the dresser was shattered, with pieces of glass scattered on the top. The bed was stripped, and aside from a few books on the desk, everything appeared in order. Her sister was either as neat as a pin, or someone had come in and cleaned.

Rosco crouched near the bed. Her gaze followed his. "Did you find something?"

"Blood." He pointed to the spots on the carpet. They made a trail to the door, and they followed them out to the bathroom. There were markers on the floor. The police would have caught them, too.

"They must have taken her bed sheets for evidence." Emma moved closer to the closet, pushed the broken mirrored door to the side, and sighed.

"Anything missing?" Rosco asked.

"I wouldn't know, but her backpack is missing."

Over by the desk, Emma spotted the framed picture of the two sisters. Another of Audra's father holding her as a child, and another of a guy Audra had dated in high school. She reached for the frame and stopped herself.

"Anybody you know?" Rosco stood close behind her. She

could feel his body heat radiating at her back. She almost leaned against him, yearning for the warmth and security she'd felt in his embrace in her office.

"That one is Audra and me. It was taken a few years ago. The other is her father, Clay, and her when she was younger."

"I meant that one," Rosco said.

She hadn't realized her hand remained outstretched and let it drop. "Isaac. They went to high school together. He committed suicide their senior year."

It was the first time Audra had come to her and cried. The first time Audra came seeking a big sister and support—not the monetary kind. She'd cried with her, and they'd made a plan for Audra's life. The one including her going to school, having a business of her own, and living a life Isaac would have wanted.

Her heart broke for her sister, for the young man who couldn't battle his manic-depressive side any longer.

Emma turned away, blinking back more tears. Where had they all come from?

Out in the living room, Cassy and her boyfriend sat with their books.

"Thank you for letting me in and for the information. I appreciate your help," she said.

"Do you think Audra will be coming back? She's not dead or anything, right?" Cassy asked.

"I wish I knew," Emma said. In her heart, she wouldn't believe her sister was gone. In trouble, yes, but not gone. *Please, Lord, help us find Audra. I'll be a better sister. Give me another chance. If not for me, for Isaac.* She pleaded, not knowing if God would listen this time.

"Let me know. Stacey wants to move in, and she can't do that if Audra is coming back."

"You'll have to leave my sister's things in her room until the end of the semester or I return to take care of them,"

Emma said. "Do you know if the police cleaned up the room?"

"They took trash bags of stuff. They even swabbed the bathroom. "

"I wonder if that's where she had the baby," Rosco murmured as they left.

For the first time since Audra's disappearance, the shock of the possibility of her sister in danger froze her.

Rosco opened the truck door for her, but Emma held onto it. "You need to tell me what you know about those men."

————

An hour later, Rosco had returned Emma to her car and insisted he follow her home. She was quiet and pale on the ride back from the college apartment complex.

He followed her to a small house in the Westmont section of town. He pulled up along the street and waited for her to go inside. She got out and headed toward him. He rolled down his window.

"Do you want to come inside?"

Most people would stay up for many hours yet, but his mornings started at four. "Are you sure?"

"I have leftover chili if you're hungry."

"How can I say no to an offer like that?" He got out of the truck and followed her. "I won't stay long. It's almost close to my bedtime."

She laughed, as he hoped she would. She had her bag with her files, and inside her home his boots clipped on hard-wood floors. The beige walls and wood trim doorways greeted him.

She tossed her keys on the table near the stairs and motioned for him to follow her into the kitchen.

"I don't bite," she said.

He grinned. "And here I figured you would be the one afraid of me."

She glanced back over her shoulder at him. Those thick lashes of hers hid her eyes as they fluttered for a moment. Slowly, the color returned to her cheeks, and she put her bag down on the counter. She motioned for him to take a seat at the island. Soft yellow walls and more natural wood met him in the kitchen. She pulled out a bowl and started dividing the leftover chili in two. "Coffee?"

"Water if you have it."

She gave him an amused look. Putting the bowls in the microwave to heat, she pulled down two glasses and filled them with water. "No caffeine after a certain time?"

"A man has got to get his beauty rest," he winked.

Her cheeks turned pink. She grabbed spoons and napkins and put them on the island in front of him.

"I want to know about this biker gang my sister was hanging out with. I need to know where to find them so that I can find my sister."

"Hold up, Emma. You should let the police handle it. The Sharks aren't the kind of men you want to mess with."

"They're bikers. How scary can they be?" She leaned against the counter, waiting for the microwave to beep.

"Scary," he said.

"You're not scary."

The microwave beeped and she got the bowls out, careful to use hot pads as she carried one to him.

"That's because I learned to behave. These guys don't follow anyone's rules but their own. Pike's been a pain in my club's butt for a while. We think he might have had something to do with an accident a friend of mine had. Charlie, the guy Audra was staying with and helping, someone messed with his ride. We think Pike put Audra up to helping sabotage our annual club rally and trying to take it over."

Emma sat the second bowl down on the other side of the island. "And you want me to believe you're not like them?"

He heard the distrust in her voice. Held his breath and stared at her while he waited for her to tell him to leave.

"I'm a sinner like everyone else. I understand what it's like to get caught in the crossfires of wanting to belong and trying to prove yourself."

She seemed to consider his response. He stood, pulled around the other stool. "Or do you prefer to stand while you eat?"

It made him uncomfortable with her standing on the other side of him.

"Tell me?" It was a question, more than a command. Emma took the seat and blew on the chili. That extra minute made it slightly warmer than comfortable to swallow.

"Got caught up with the wrong people telling me to do the wrong things." Rosco shrugged. "Do the crime, pay the time, as my father would say."

"My father would tell me the same thing. Although, I think the worst I ever did was sneak out of the house when I was sixteen."

"Bet that went over well," he said.

She took a sip of her water. "Depends on whose point of view. I never figured my father would find me or drag me back home. Talk about embarrassing. He didn't even have to ground me. I was too mortified to show my face around my newfound friends after that, and they probably figured friendship with me was too much trouble."

"I take it your dad showed up to a party."

She made a face. "Oh yeah. Caught me on Billy Kemp's lap and our faces plastered together. Needless to say, no boy would date me the rest of high school."

"Fathers can be pretty scary." He took a mouthful of chili and tried not to moan at how spicy it tasted. This girl liked

things hot. Good thing she'd given him a tall glass of water to
wash it down.

"As if you would know?" she scoffed.

He shook his head. "I've encountered a few angry
fathers."

When she gave him that disbelieving look, he put his
hands on his chest. "Hey, I might be a guy, but a dude knows
you can't sneak around with a man's daughter and always get
away with it."

She laughed.

"You didn't think it was funny when you got caught,"
Rosco pointed out, loving her laugh. It sent warm tendrils
under his skin, watching her eyes shine with the secret behind
her humor. He couldn't help wondering what she was thinking
and wanting to laugh along with her. Was it the picture of a
younger version of him getting grabbed by the scruff of the
neck and tossed from a make-out session with a girl, or was it
her memories?

"No. I don't suppose I did. Mortified, more like it. But for
the guy, I'm sure it terrified him. He never came near me
again, or it gave him a boost of reputation and he moved on."

"Terrified." Rosco reached across the table and took her
hand. "Any guy would be crazy to kiss you and not want to
come back for more."

She blushed. It was cute. Pink swept over her cheeks and
went up to her ears. She glanced away, and he cleared his
throat, realizing he said more than he should have, but his
mouth had spoken out loud for his mind.

She withdrew her hands, tucking a piece of hair back
behind her ear. "I should let you eat. I wouldn't want you to
fall asleep on your drive home."

"I'm good, but I know you have work to do."

"Yeah."

"Do you always get up early and have long days?" she
asked.

"Mostly. When you work for family, the job is never done."
He stood up and put his empty water glass and bowl in the
sink.

"Thank you for the chili."

"Sure thing."

"See you tomorrow?" He didn't want her getting it in her
head to go searching for Pike or any of the Sharks on
her own.

"Oh. I'm not sure. I need to get Isaac's room ready before
the social worker arrives for the home inspection. Other than
a crib, I have no idea what he'll need."

"Don't worry. I think I can help with that."

"You're just full of baby knowledge, aren't you?"

"Comes from having nephews and nieces. How about I
see you around lunch? We can grab a bite to eat and do some
shopping."

She bit her lip, and he wondered if she would turn him
down. "I planned on coming back to check on Isaac. I have
court tomorrow. Maybe when I get off work? I'm not sure—"

"No" wasn't in his vocabulary. "Five like today, but be
warned, I fall asleep around nine." He gave her his best smile.
"Four in the morning comes early."

"I'll meet you at the hospital," she said.

She hadn't kicked him out as she suspected other women
might have from his past. He would take seeing her tomorrow.
It would give him time to talk to the other club members and
stop in to see Haden or Charlie. He wanted to find Audra
almost as much as Emma did. A baby deserved to have a
loving family, but more than that, it was one thing to give up a
baby and another thing to make sure all parties were safe.

If Pike had his guys out looking for Audra, then maybe
she was in more trouble than Emma realized. Emma might
not be safe if Pike and his gang knew she was looking for
Audra. He remembered what happened to Holly and the

thought of Pike putting his hands on Emma sent a burn through his chest.

So far, from what he learned about Audra, she seemed like a mixed-up young woman, and he remembered what it was like at that age. He just hoped they could find her in time to help her.

"See you tomorrow."

He shoved down the urge to pull her into his arms. Rosco wished he could lift the burdens sagging on her shoulders and making her lips turn down. He took a long, hard look at them and shook any ideas of wanting to kiss her aside.

Too soon, he thought as she opened the door to him tonight. He wouldn't rush in like a fool. They both needed time to get to know one another first. Find her sister. Keep her safe.

It didn't lessen the pull inside him to reach out and brush his thumb down the tear stain on her cheek showing through the powder she used trying to cover it.

Once she closed the door, Rosco pulled out his phone and made some calls as he walked to his vehicle. He got the feeling Emma had gotten used to doing things on her own. Well, not anymore.

8

Emma buried her head in her hands for a moment. She couldn't think after staying up all night. It had gotten that way since Audra went missing. She woke up several times thinking she heard her phone ring. She'd drift off to sleep and wake again, never letting her body fully fall into a deep slumber. Each time, it was her mind playing tricks on her.

This morning, she'd called the hospital to check on baby Isaac. The nurse reported he was still the same. It was good. He was alive and getting stronger. She'd speak with the doctor again today to check on Isaac's progress, to be sure, and see if her nephew needed anything else to ensure his recovery.

She heard the soft click of her office door, figured it was Lori bringing her another stack of files for the Bennett case. Peering up through her fingers, she startled. A man in biker gear leaned back against the closed door. His dirty blond hair spiked, most likely from the wind of his ride, and an earring of a cross dangled from one ear.

"C-Can I help you?" She lowered her hands, sat back in her chair, but kept her hand close to her phone beside her keyboard.

"Emma Harris?" The man kept his voice low. His gaze

shifted to the glass by the door, and he kept his body against the frame. No one could look inside and see she had company.

"I am. And you are?" She couldn't help the icy feeling seeping into her fingertips as they edged toward her phone. "Do we have an appointment?" she asked.

He held up his hands. "No, but I have a message for you."

"How did you get past the front secretary?" Her eyes fell to the patch on his vest.

He frowned, his gaze followed hers, and then he lowered his hands. "All I can say is that I have my ways."

He said it as if it should amuse her, but several warning bells went off in her head. She curled her hand around her phone.

He must have sensed her panic, for he said, "She's safe."

His words took her off guard.

"Excuse me?"

He pointed to the phone. "You don't need to call anyone, Ms. Harris. I'm sorry you feel threatened, but your sister asked me to make sure you knew she was safe."

"My s-sister?" The surprise made her stutter.

"Audra," he spoke softly.

Emma gasped. "You know where my sister is? Tell me! She's in trouble, isn't she?" she said, muttering more to herself than him.

"Of course she's in trouble, and she knows it."

She jumped to her feet. "Tell me where she is."

He shook his head, a deepening frown, and etchings between his eyes. "I can't. All I can tell you is that she's safe. For now. Don't go looking for her."

"Oh? And why not? You can't just abandon your child and take off! Who are you anyway?"

He glanced again at the window by the door. Emma's voice rose and, most likely, anyone outside her door could hear. She took a deep breath, trying to calm down. She couldn't let him take off without getting answers first. How did this man know Audra, and why was he helping her?

"Who are you?"

"I'm a friend. I told her this was a bad idea, but she assured me I could trust you."

"Audra said that?" Her sister had put more faith in her than she suspected. Then again, Audra would, being in trouble and needing someone to get her out. She'd learned that from Deb.

"Yeah. Why don't you sit down?" He waved his hand for her to sit.

"Why don't you?" Emma indicated the seat across from her desk.

"It's better if I stand right here."

Emma's vision narrowed, and she held onto the phone, clutching it in front of her. "You're one of them?"

"Who?" the man asked, then nodded toward her. "If you don't sit down, someone will look in and think it odd."

He had a point, Emma thought as she sat down, keeping her hands on her lap along with her phone.

"Keep the phone up where I can see it. I don't need you texting anyone," he said.

She bit her lip and put the phone up on her desk. He didn't appear armed, but his commanding tone added to her unease.

Soon Lori would come with those court files she asked to be pulled.

"Happy? Now, are you going to tell me who you are?"

"They call me Beast," he said.

"You're one of those biker gang guys my sister was hanging out with?"

"You know about that?"

She debated on how much to tell him. Her silence must have shown her reserve, for he said, "You were right to assume your sister is in trouble. She's lucky to be alive, and I'd like to keep her that way."

"So, are you the father of Audra's baby?" she asked.

His eyes widened, the muscle under his jaw twitched. He shook his head.

"Why should I believe you? Any of this? If you're a friend of my sister's, then we should call the police." Her fingers itched to dial the detective in charge of her sister's missing person case.

"The police are aware. They are handling it."

"If they know my sister is alive and where she is, then why wouldn't they have told me? Or a family member? There are laws against child abandonment."

She worked with the system every day, all too aware of the laws and how to protect innocent child victims. Never in her life had she figured she'd have to deal with a case involving her own family. It shouldn't have come as a shock. Audra was and always would be like their mother.

"It's complicated. The police will not tell you anything that could put the case at risk. There is more going on than you realize, counselor," he said.

"More than you can tell me?" Her hands shook, and she clasped them together.

"Just coming here has possibly compromised my position."

"In the gang?"

"You mentioned friends. Has someone been around asking you questions?" he asked.

"Why should I tell you?" She couldn't help the heat balling her belly. The police knew Audra was alive? Did this guy think her a fool? "How do I know you're telling me the truth? You could be fishing for information like the others."

"I take it these friends had patches like this one?" He turned and indicated the back of his vest.

"Of course."

He reached up and ran a hand over his scuffed jaw. "Listen, if those friends of mine come back, call and let the police know. Don't tell them anything. Otherwise, your sister will show up dead somewhere, just like her baby."

His eyes weren't cold, but his words froze her in place. "Are you threatening me?"

"I'm trying to keep your sister alive."

Emma blinked. The relief of knowing her sister was alive rushed forward along with the twisted fact Isaac should have been dead.

"Is that why she abandoned her baby?"

"I have to go. I'm sorry for your loss, but at least you have the comfort of knowing your sister is alive. They have someone watching the hospital and clinics around town. I've seen you coming and going there almost daily. A client?"

"You could say that." She decided it best not to tell him about Isaac. Did Audra believe her baby was dead?

Would telling her the truth change the current situation?

She saw movement outside the door. "My assistant will be coming in any moment with files I requested. If you see my sister, will you give her a message?"

He scowled but nodded.

"Tell her Isaac lives."

"Isaac lives?" he said, so softly she almost didn't hear him.

"She should know." If it were her, she'd want to know. What Audra did with the information was up to her. Would it bring her relief or more torment for the trouble she was in? That, Emma didn't know. Her imagination ran wild with the possibilities.

Oh, Lord. What has my sister gotten herself into? Please keep her safe, no matter what. She's still my sister.

Behind the rough exterior, the shock smoothed out on his face. He swallowed hard. "Who else knows?"

"The police. I believe it was in the paper yesterday about the baby found behind the campus apartments."

"Your client?"

"In a matter of speaking," she said.

She'd distracted him long enough for the door to rattle behind him with the turn of the knob. Lori had a habit of not knocking. He jumped to the side as the door opened so that Lori wouldn't see him at first.

"I could find all but one. I think Jacob Marrow has it. I can ask him for it when he's finished." Lori unloaded the files on Emma's desk.

"That would be great. Thanks."

Lori turned, startled. Her hand went to her heart. "I didn't realize you had someone in with you. I'm sorry. There weren't any appointments on your schedule until later." Her gaze traveled between Beast and Emma.

"I was just leaving." Beast walked around the door and left. Emma wanted to go after him. He still hadn't told her what kind of trouble Audra was in, but it was the killing kind.

She sat deeper in her seat. Maybe telling them Isaac was alive had been a bad idea. Someone wanted her sister dead, and it made her sick to her stomach.

Lori stared after him. Her fingers still clutching her blouse as she turned and looked at Emma. "What did he want? How did he get past Mary Lou?"

Emma shook her head, trying to focus.

"Should I call security?" Lori asked.

Emma held out her hand. "No. It's okay. He was bringing me information."

Audra. Her sister. Was alive.

———

Sebastian knew he'd taken a chance by tracking down Audra's sister. It hadn't been hard once Audra had given him her name.

She'd assured him at the hotel no one else knew she had a sister. He walked down the sidewalk, cut across and between the buildings before coming out on another street closer to where he'd parked his motorcycle. He pulled up the collar of his jacket to keep the chill off his neck.

Pike had assigned another guppy and two of his officers to scout around to find Audra. If her dead body didn't show up soon, Pike would put a bounty on her head.

Inside a local coffee shop, he waited his turn at the counter. This part of town drew in an eclectic group of people. Not far from the college campus, many students came here to study. He glanced around, waiting for his order.

"Are you sure you don't want the whipped topping?" the barista asked him.

A curvy thing with a smile twice as wide. She inflicted an instant jolt of joy that became contagious.

"Do I look like a whipped kind of guy?"

She laughed and slid him the large foam cup with a lid. "Not even a little sugar?"

She batted her lashes, and he gave in to a little flirting. It kept him at the counter where he scoped the place out. A group of women sat on the couch and chairs toward the back against the bookcases. To his right, a dude and a girl talked and shared a scone.

"Your smile is enough to sweeten anyone up," he winked.

She giggled and turned away for a moment to grab another order. Sebastian spied the paper someone discarded on a chair nearby. He scooped it up, holding his straight-up black coffee, and looked at the top spread of news.

He noticed a few people had given him uncomfortable glances. The barista came around the corner. "Sad, isn't it?"

He read the news heading, saw the photo, and grimaced. "Mind if I take this?"

She shrugged, sidling up to him a little closer. "It's yesterday's news."

His flirting mood disappeared. "Thanks. I'll see you around."

She opened her mouth to protest. She held a napkin in her hand, and Beast had the feeling she was about to give him her number. Too bad. Out of everyone in the quirky little coffee shop, she hadn't been discouraged by his attire.

Outside, Chum stood by his motorbike. "Since when does a man go in for coffee?"

"Since the bar doesn't open until later," Sebastian said. "What you doing? Following me?"

"Pike's looking for you. He doesn't like you're not at his beck and call like the rest of us." Chum walked his fingers up the handlebars of Sebastian's ride. Small hairs rose on his neck.

"Is that right?"

"Yep," Chum said.

"Well, then I guess we should go see him. He'll want to know what I found."

Chum's shoulders rolled back. "You took off before scrubbing the floors."

"But you did. I'll make sure you get the credit, too." Sebastian waved the paper.

"What you got?" Chum asked.

"Yesterday's news."

Sebastian mounted his motorcycle. Tucking the paper inside his vest, he took a long swig of his coffee. He would need it facing Pike. So far, he'd been able to stay under the club president's radar since the kidnapping incident where he helped the daughter of Pike's rival escape.

The DA was putting pressure on him to dig in deeper. Keeping Audra safe hadn't been part of the plan, and now he had no choice. More than one life hung on the line if he failed.

There was no going back.

Chum followed him to the Sharks' compound. An old truck garage converted to house members and worked-on motorcycles. It had become more of a chop shop operation, and Sebastian suspected drug smuggling along with stolen parts. As a guppy, he had to earn his ranks in the club. Earning rank would also earn him privileges to information on where the club had dealings and with whom.

He never figured Pike would kidnap Holly Brooks, or that Pike's old lady, Audra, would have the heart to help her escape. Without his intervention, Holly wouldn't have made it out of the neighborhood alive.

He hadn't counted on Pike finding out Audra's part in launching the escape. She had the courage. He'd give her that. The kind of courage that could get someone killed. Maybe kill them both.

He parked his ride along with the other motorcycles outside the bar area of the building. Tonight the doors would open, and the regulars would pour in. Behind the bar, the club would hold church, and the noise of the chop shop would become music and rowdy patrons.

Inside the building, Chum followed close behind Sebastian as he went down the hall for Pike's office. Moray, a guy with a long tattoo of an eel on his neck, stood by the door.

"Boss in?" Sebastian asked.

"What you guppies doing here? Aren't you supposed to be scrubbing the floor?" Moray crossed his arms.

"I got news for the boss. He'll want to see it."

Moray held out his hand, and Sebastian handed him the newspaper.

Moray snorted. "Get back to scrubbing. Pike don't read no papers."

"He will when it has to do with Dory."

At the mention of Audra's club name, Moray made a face. He snatched the paper from Sebastian.

"Campus news."

Moray nodded, flung the paperback at him. "What makes you think he doesn't know?"

Sebastian shrugged. "I know he's got Puffer and Tiger out

trying to find her. Figured this might give him a clue." He ignored the tightening in his gut.

Moray reached back and knocked on the door while keeping his eyes on Sebastian.

Several raps of his knuckles and the door yanked open. "This better be good. I said no disturbances!" Pike held open the door. His body was taking up space. His beard was split into two braids.

"Guppy brought you some news."

Chum stepped back as Pike's eyes landed on him. Sebastian held open the newspaper. Pike grabbed it. He grunted as his eyes scanned the photo and the headline. "Dead baby in the trash. So? You think this is news I care about?"

The paper didn't say the baby was dead, just found and taken to Conemaugh Hospital.

Sebastian played it cool. "My bad. I figured it happened near Dory's place. Might help find her."

Pike's face reddened. "How do you know where that treacherous shrew lives?"

"I heard Puffer talking with Tiger. I figured I could help. Didn't mean to overstep."

Pike's eyes turned dark, and the man balled his fist. Paper crumpling and ripping echoed in the hall's silence.

"When I find her, I'll kill her. Not you. Or you. Or you." Pike pointed at each man. "She's mine."

Pike stepped back, slammed the door. Behind him, Chum stiffened. "Don't go soiling yourself, man. Just finish cleaning the floor."

Sebastian turned and headed back down the hallway. Pike confirmed his suspicions. Eventually, another member of the Sharks would come across the paper or hear the news and pass it on to their leader.

Emma had every reason to fear for her sister's life.

Pike's old lady was a dead woman, in more ways than one.

"Where you think you're going?" Moray called.

"Floors, remember?" Beast called back.

The VP of the Sharks grunted.

"That was stupid," Chum grumbled, catching up to him. "Pike has killed men for less."

He had a bad feeling his fellow prospect was right.

9

After Emma's encounter with the biker guy in her office, she again called the detective on her sister's case.

"I'm sorry, Ms. Harris. In cases like these, it's difficult. I don't want to give you false hope."

"Just tell me that my sister is alive."

He sighed on the other end of the line.

"Please," she whispered, a tear escaping her eye. "I think other people are looking for her."

There was a pause, sounds of papers and keyboards and faraway chatter. "What makes you think that? Has someone come to see you?"

She tapped her fingers on her desk for a moment. "A guy with one of those biker gang vests on. And Audra's roommate told me they were at her apartment asking questions about her, too."

"You went to her apartment again?"

"Of course, she's my sister. I wanted to check on her roommate. On her stuff." Partially true.

"Listen, if those guys come around you again, call me. Otherwise, please stay away from them. We're looking into this. Let us do our job."

"Fine." She hung up as Lori knocked on the door and announced she was heading out for lunch. That was Emma's signal to head out, too. She needed to check on Isaac, and she looked forward to seeing Rosco.

Instead of driving over to the hospital, she took an Uber, remembering the man's warning that they were checking hospitals. They didn't know Audra had a sister, but would they notice her coming every day, or Rosco? What if she asked him not to wear his vest when he came? Would it insult him?

Once the Uber driver dropped her off, she glanced around, paranoid if anyone watched her. She clung to the strap of her purse and tried to keep her steps normal. A part of her wanted to race inside the building and hurry to make sure Isaac was still there, safe and alive.

Inside the lobby, Rosco stood holding a flower, a single chrysanthemum, the cheery shade of yellow.

"You're here already? Why didn't you go up?"

"I wanted to wait for you. I picked this from my mother's garden. Figured it would brighten your day."

"How did you know chrysanthemums are my favorite?" she asked, taking the flower.

"I didn't, but I had a feeling."

They walked together to the elevators, and inside she told him of her unusual visitor. Never had she blurted things out to someone like that, maybe because she hadn't had many relationships with men or felt comfortable enough around them as she did Rosco.

"You said his name was Beast?"

She nodded, watching the numbers light up on the elevator.

"You can trust him."

She glanced over at him. "You know him."

"I don't know what he's doing with the Sharks. But I know he's a good guy."

"He said Audra is alive."

"Then you should believe him." Rosco put his hand against her back to usher her out of the elevator. The nurse offered Rosco a gown to cover his clothes to go in with Emma to the NICU. "It's always nice to see both parents loving on their little one," she said.

"Oh, no. No. We're not. I mean, he's not," Emma stammered.

"We're just friends," Rosco said.

"I'm the aunt," Emma felt the need to clarify.

"Then do you two have permission to be inside here?" she questioned.

"If you check, you'll see both our names," Emma assured the nurse, who she hadn't seen in the NICU before. The dark-skinned woman double-checked, and Emma appreciated her following up for Isaac's protection.

Inside, Emma and Rosco sat beside him, her hand inside the tiny incubator. His long, thin fingers curled around her pinky.

"He's got you now," Rosco teased. "He'll try to get away with everything when he's older."

"You think so?" She basked in his nearness. Shoulder to shoulder, they sat with little Isaac holding onto her finger. He'd been sleeping, and she hadn't wanted to disturb him. Tiny wisps of hair, so soft, coated his little head. When his eyes opened for a few moments, Emma thought her heart would melt and stick to him forever.

They sat like that for over an hour—Rosco at her side, Emma with Isaac's tiny hand around her finger, and never wanting to leave this place or moment.

Soon a nurse came with a bottle, and they took him out of the incubator. Emma held him to feed him. He ate so little at a time, and she marveled at how he could be content with it.

Her watch buzzed, a reminder she needed to return to the office, back to her files, and to the waiting meeting she had with a young child's mother who decided that letting the foster parents adopt was better for the child.

Outside the NICU, Rosco walked beside her, when she spotted Janet Summers.

"It's good to see you again," Janet said.

"Are you here checking up on my nephew, Ms. Summers?" Emma asked, suddenly feeling defensive.

"Guilty as charged, but I was here on another case down in the emergency room and decided while I was here to see how he's been doing."

"That's kind of you," Rosco said.

"I don't believe we've met." Janet hugged her iPad against her. The woman appeared to carry it everywhere.

"Rosco Reynolds." Rosco held out his hand, and Janet shook it.

"Rosco was the one who found Isaac and called 911," Emma said.

"My driver Melvin did the calling, but I found him."

Janet fiddled with her scarf, the corner of her lips lifting. "You're a trash man? That must have been a surprise for you, finding a baby like that."

"His family owns the company," Emma interjected in the conversation, her defensive mechanism refusing to turn off.

"Let's say finding a baby was a way more pleasant surprise than some other things I've encountered," Rosco said, chuckling.

"I'm sure," Janet said, tilting her head and looking at Emma with interest. "Are you ready for my visit tomorrow?"

"Tomorrow?" Had it been a week already?

"Yes. Tomorrow," Janet said.

She still needed a crib. She had done no shopping besides ordering a few things online. They should arrive by the weekend, but tomorrow?

Emma bit the inside of her cheek, counting to ten, then replied, "Of course."

"Good. I'll see you tomorrow afternoon. Two o'clock."

"Looking forward to it," Emma said, watching the social worker walk away.

"You're not ready, are you?" Rosco asked once the social worker disappeared down the hallway.

Emma shook her head. "I know I had to do it. I started clearing out the room, but this week has been crazy with worrying about Audra, Isaac, and work."

He placed his arm around her shoulder and squeezed. "I get it. We'll start with a crib. Did you buy one yet?"

She shook her head. She'd looked at dozens of them online. Who knew cribs came in so many colors, shapes, and features? She liked the dark-colored one that would convert to a toddler bed later, but then she'd stop herself and remind herself that this wasn't her baby. And would Audra ever come back to be a mother to him?

She couldn't set herself up for the hurt. Even now, she asked God what she'd gotten herself into.

"I've got my truck. We'll go to Walmart. They sell cribs and baby stuff."

"I have a meeting at two thirty. I don't have time to go shopping."

"Leave it to me. What color do you want? I think they come in brown or white. I'll pick it up, and I'll swing by your place after work and put it together."

"Oh." She couldn't let him do that. Could she? Tomorrow was Friday. She only worked half a day. "Um..." She chewed her lip.

"Hey, pick a color. I got this."

"At least let me give you money to pay for it." She went to open her purse.

"We'll square up later. Color or do I get to choose?" He stared right into her eyes. His face was so close. She could smell his faint cologne the entire time they'd sat together with

Isaac. Her belly did a little flop, and her gaze dropped to his lips. "How about I buy whichever one they have?"

He moved away, herding her inside the elevator. She hadn't even heard it open.

"I'm not sure about that." She pulled out her phone. She saw too many reports of babies getting hurt in cribs and wanted her nephew to be safe. She pulled up the app for the store and browsed the selection: two different cribs, two different color choices.

"I like that one." Rosco pointed to her phone.

"I do too, but I want the dark-colored one," she admitted.

"One cherry—" He squinted to see her phone better. "Slumber baby crib."

"Does it come with a mattress?" She tried scrolling. Was it like a regular bed? How was she supposed to know? She'd never had a baby.

"Nope. I'll get you one."

"Tonight then? I can order it here and put your name on it to pick it up." Yes, she decided to do that. She paused outside in the lobby, taking enough time to order the crib for pickup, thankful they had it in store. "Pickup after four o'clock," she said.

"I'll be there." He gave her his email address for her to forward the receipt for pickup.

"Thank you." They walked out of the hospital together.

"Where did you park?" he asked.

"I took an Uber. I was afraid after Beast came to see me that someone would follow me or know my car. He said they're watching the hospitals and clinics."

"I'll give you a lift, no need for an Uber."

"You don't have to do that."

"I know," he said. "I want to."

Once they reached his truck, Rosco held open the door for her. A tiny flutter rippled in her belly as she got in. She gave him the address and watched out the window as he drove.

Quietly, she tried to digest everything over the past several hours. A few times, she chanced a glance his way, felt as if he watched her, but then his eyes were on the direction ahead. Far too soon, it felt, the ride had ended.

He allowed her to slip out and wished her a good rest of the day. Her eyes veered to his lips, and the flutter from before reoccurred. She walked as fast as she could without appearing rude or like she wanted to get away from him. She hadn't, but she had at the same time.

Not thinking, she skipped the elevator and took the curved stairs around the water fountain in the center of the building up to the third floor to her office. On her desk, a sticky note with bold black letters awaited her. URGENT.

Taking a minute to get her bearings and brain back to work, Emma sank into her chair. *Just breathe. Audra's alive. Isaac is coming home soon. A relationship will only make things worse. Focus, Emma. You have clients who need you.*

Emma placed her hand on the URGENT note. She bowed her head and took a moment to pray over it, as she did most of her cases. She knew whatever lay ahead, God would help her handle it.

10

On his way home, Rosco stopped by the motorcycle shop to see Haden. An array of toasted leaves of dark brown and gold crunched under his feet as he approached the garage. Inside, he heard the sounds of metal clank against metal.

Music blared from the stereo, and Rosco ducked his head into the office. Empty. Disappointed, he turned back inside the garage as Haden spotted him and came closer. "You're late for lunch. It's good to see you."

"Same."

He followed Haden over to a toolbox. In the back of the shop, the sounds of blaring music died, and the station changed. Haden made a face, yelled, "Yo. I'm still here. Change it back."

Not a second later, the station returned to the original rock blaring, and Haden shook his head, chuckling.

"How's it going?" Rosco asked.

"These teenagers think they know everything and try to get away with anything. Nothing I haven't already tried. Ty's not bad. I got him through the internship program at the vocational school, but he likes to figure out things on his own, which isn't the best way."

"Sounds like someone else I know."

Haden grinned. "Didn't think I'd see you until Saturday at breakfast. What's up?"

"I came by hoping to see your woman. Holly around?" Rosco asked.

"She's out running errands. Something about a dress fitting and checking in with a caterer. Not sure if it's for our wedding or someone else's bash. I can't keep track. She's got it all color-coded in that planner she likes to carry."

"I'm happy for you."

"You're not trying to back out of best man duties, are you?" Haden narrowed his gaze.

Rosco laughed, shook his head, and said, "I'll be there."

"Good, Hols has got you hooked up with her cousin Natalie on her mother's side. She's single and works as a secretary at a school out near Squirrel Hill."

"Since when did Holly move from event planning to matchmaker?" Rosco fiddled with a socket laying atop the toolbox.

"Since I told her you were available and hadn't had a serious relationship since high school."

"You think you're getting married, the rest of us should get hitched, too?"

How long before Holly and Haden started a family after they got married? Would Rosco end up the bachelor friend who became an uncle to everyone else's kids because he had none of his own?

Little Isaac came to mind, and Emma, with her arms around that small baby, his tiny fingers wrapped around Emma's index finger. His chest filled up and stretched.

His buddy did not know how blessed he was to have Holly and the plans of a future underway.

"You're saying that when Jess got married, she didn't try hooking you up with some ex of her husband's?"

"They were still friends, and Sean wanted me to distract

her from doing anything to stress Jess out on their special day."

Haden smirked, grabbed another tool, and headed back to the Suzuki without a front wheel. "Sounds like a setup."

"I don't need a setup. I can find a date on my own."

"Well, for the wedding party, you're stuck with Natalie. Afterward, bring a date."

"Don't mind if I do." Rosco shoved his hands in his back pockets. "That's part of the reason I came to see you."

Haden crouched down by the bike. He looked up at Rosco. "To ask Holly to bring a date?"

"To ask Holly to plan a party."

Haden rested a hand on his knee. "What kind of party?"

"The social worker is coming to inspect Emma's house before Emma can bring Isaac home. She needs help. I thought you and Holly could come over. We'll put together the crib, and women are always better at knowing what they need for these kinds of things. I'll ask Nicole, she said she could gather some clothes, and I'm sure some women from the club know about buying diapers."

"When?"

"Tonight."

Haden whistled. "Cutting it close."

"Isaac's mother is Audra, Haden. I figured Holly would want to help."

A glint came into his eye, and his jaw tightened. It lasted a moment, enough for Rosco to regret mentioning Audra's name and reminding Haden of Holly's kidnapping. "I'm sorry, man. I shouldn't have mentioned it."

"No." Haden reached in his pocket, pulled out his phone. He touched the screen, and Rosco could hear the ringing.

"Hey, Hols, change of plans for tonight. It looks like we're going to a baby shower. Can you call up Judy and invite a few ladies to help?"

A few moments later, Haden hung up after going over the

details. They would meet at Emma's place. All he needed to
do was get the crib and talk to his sister, Nicole.

"See you at seven."

"Wouldn't miss it. I can't wait to meet your girl."

"She's not my girl."

Haden shrugged. "You like her."

And that Rosco could agree with. He liked Emma Harris
—a little too much.

"I'll be there, but I'll make sure I let her know you're
coming. She got a visit from Beast this morning, and it
spooked her. I think this whole thing with Audra missing has
weighed on her."

Haden called for Ty to get him a new tire out of the back.
Rosco did not know how the kid heard so well with the music
turned up in the garage area.

"Beast? You saw him?" Haden asked.

"No. Emma said he called himself Beast. She described
him. I don't know what he's doing with the Sharks, but I'm
guessing he's trying to find evidence against Pike after what he
did to Charlie. I figured they would have arrested him after he
tried to kidnap Holly."

Haden stood, going to see where Ty was with that tire,
Rosco suspected. He followed him to see if he could help.

"Didn't try. He took her. It was my fault. If I would have
picked her up for the wedding or gone sooner…"

"Let's not go back there. You're going to be seeing her at
your wedding in a few months," Rosco said.

Haden grunted. He walked to the storage area of the
garage. Ty stood looking at the tires.

"The 712s."

Ty, a young man with jet black hair and round face, looked
back at them. "I don't think we have any."

Rosco waited while Haden searched. "Okay, I'll see we get
them ordered. I thought I had one left."

"You put it on Ace's ride the other day."

Haden scratched his jaw. "Right then. I'll be in the office."

Rosco kept his mouth shut. Inside the office, Haden reached for papers on the desk. "Listen, if she saw Beast, then you can't tell her he's a cop. We have to protect his cover."

"You knew then?"

"His ride is here, and I lent him one of ours from the lot. He said he was disappearing for a bit. I didn't ask, but if he's with the Sharks, then he's undercover. They tried arresting Pike, but it was Hols' word against his and the rest of his gang."

"Now Emma and Audra and the baby. I have a bad feeling about all this. I hope Beast knows what he's gotten himself into."

"You and me both. They couldn't hold Pike for taking Hols, but if I know Beast, the authorities are digging deeper, and I hope they put an end to the Sharks before anyone else gets hurt."

"Especially now that it involves women and children," Rosco half-muttered.

Haden clasped Rosco on the shoulder. "You going to be able to stay awake for a late-night party?"

Rosco snorted. "It's at seven o'clock."

Haden glanced over to watch Ty sort through tools in another box just outside the office.

"I'm heading home to take a nap, and I told Brian I'd help weld and repair some dumpsters. I need to pick up the crib and meet Emma at her place. I'll text you the address."

"Sounds like you better pick up some caffeine while you're at it."

Rosco rolled back his shoulders. "I might stop in at the coffee place again. Nicole likes that frou-frou coffee. It'll butter her up."

"Manipulation by caffeine? You're the bro." Haden moved to go around the desk.

"Maybe you should try that on Holly."

"Oh, I've got other ways with Hols." Haden grinned.

Rosco waved him off, not wanting to think of those other ways Haden used to woo Holly into getting his way. Heat slipped up his neck, picturing Emma in his arms. Man, he must be tired. Rosco headed back to his apartment above his family's garbage disposal company. As soon as Brian spotted his truck, he'd get no rest. The frou-frou coffee got forgotten in the tangle of his thoughts.

He planned to snooze for an hour or two, tops, until he felt the shove of his shoulder and woke with a start on the couch. Nicole glared at him, her arms crossed and her foot tapping. "Sleeping on the job?"

It took a moment to sit up, brush the sleep away, and look at his phone. He'd slept an hour over what he'd planned.

"Lucas said you ditched him and left him to work in the back doing repairs on his own."

Rosco stretched, cupped the back of his neck. "I'm on my way now, but I need a favor."

Her eyebrow lifted, and he waited. The sigh came next. "What kind of favor? Does it have to do with the dumpster baby?"

"Isaac. He has a name. And yes, it does."

She sat on the couch as he swung his legs out of the way. "You're getting attached."

"In a way." Admitting he might have feelings for Emma would put him at his sister's advantage. He learned a long time ago not to give his siblings firing power against him. He had this overpowering sense to protect baby Isaac and his aunt.

"Tell me how I can help," she said.

———

Two hours in front of the judge, and nothing got solved. Emma dropped her files on her desk, looked at her computer, and sighed. She picked up the laptop and stuffed it in her satchel, hoping Lori had let it finish the updates while she'd been gone from the office.

A soft rap on the door made her turn her head.

"Danvers wants to see you."

"I was just heading home." She pulled her shoulders in. The judge held the Bennett case over to give the birth mother more time to prove she could create a stable home environment for her three-year-old son. Emma had seen it before. The birth mother's attorney wanted to stretch things out, get what fees he could for defending the case, and in the end, the adoptive parents would get awarded the child. She glanced down at the files she'd dropped. Marcy and Ben Bennett were good, God-fearing people.

"You shouldn't keep him waiting."

Emma nodded, needing a minute to collect herself after the long day. "Thanks, Lori. I'll see you Monday."

"Okay, see you."

She heard Lori leave. Everything else in her office could wait. She headed down the hall to the elevator. Five o'clock and several personnel prepared to go home for the evening. Some would stay late, like Danvers.

On the fourth floor of their office building, she headed toward his office. His secretary waved her in. "He's waiting."

She tugged on her blazer and pushed back a strand of her hair.

"Ms. Harris, I've been waiting to catch you before leaving for the day. How is the Bennett case coming along?"

She stood before his desk. He motioned for her to sit. Emma took the seat closest, afraid her legs would shake. Danvers emailed her, sent his secretary out, but this time he wanted to see her.

"The judge extended the date for the birth mother to

prove stability. We'll revisit the appeal in six months. Until then, the Bennetts retain their adoptive rights to the child."

Danvers, a gentleman in his late forties, pressed his hands together. "Good. How is the Everson case?"

"Delayed." She crossed her legs, surprised Danvers knew the names of her current clients.

"How so?" he asked.

Her mouth felt dry, and she licked her lips, trying to get some moisture back to speak. "The wife filed a countersuit, and Mr. Everson's lack of proof and refusal to take a DNA test has held things back."

"Is that so?" The ridges of Mr. Danvers's forehead relaxed. "Nothing to do with canceling and rescheduling with him?"

"Once. I had a personal matter to attend to, and the appointment before Mr. Everson failed to show."

"It's been brought to my attention you have had other issues going on that might distract you from your cases. I hope it isn't anything that will keep you from doing your job. I brought you on because you're a hard worker, Ms. Harris. You can imagine my surprise when Everson came to me and requested a new lawyer to handle his case."

"I'm sorry he feels that way." Emma sat stiffly in the chair.

Losing Clinton Everson as a client wouldn't hurt her feelings. Having it brought to Danvers's attention upset her more. She swiped at a piece of lint on her blouse.

"Me too. Our clients expect us to have their best interests at heart."

Their best interests, but what about the best interests of the child? Clinton Everson wanted full custody of a child he spent no time with to get payback against a wife he'd also neglected. Emma hadn't wanted the case, but she couldn't refuse it, not when it came from one of the firm's partners.

"I have to be honest, Mr. Danvers. I'm not sure why you

assigned me to Mr. Everson's case. Had you read the files, you would see the child clearly belongs with his mother."

Danvers quirked a brow. "Have you become a judge, too?"

She bit her lip. *Good going, Emma. The last thing you need is to get fired when you have another mouth to feed.*

"No, sir. But if you read the case files, you'll see the court will find in favor of the mother. The court will give him visitation and probably even go as far as fifty-fifty custody as long as the child stays in the same school district."

"It's our job to see we do everything we can. Everson doesn't feel you're committed to his case. Under the circumstances, I believe he is right. I want you to forward his files to Jacob."

"Jacob Marrow?" She tried not to slump in the seat. "Doesn't he only handle injury cases?"

Danvers shrugged. "He has time, unlike you, Ms. Harris. I suggest you make sure you have the time for the clients you take on. This firm can't afford to have clients left hanging. You're young, and you are new, so I understand there is a learning curve. Go home. Get your priorities straight and make sure you are ready to start again on Monday."

Emma looked down at her lap. *Oh God, let this be the worst thing that happens today.* She stood, smiled, and said, "Thank you, Mr. Danvers. I appreciate your time. Let me assure you my clients' cases are important to me, and I hold them in the utmost priority."

She walked out, spotting Mary Lou down the hall, peering around the door. Emma took a deep breath and walked past the firm's front desk receptionist. A short, dark-haired woman, Mary Lou slid an envelope in the slot near the door of a paralegal working on that floor.

She avoided Mary Lou's gaze and went on her way. She wouldn't let Everson, Danvers, or Mary Lou make her day worse.

She couldn't wait to get home. Couldn't wait to see Rosco.

The notification on her phone sent an alert from the store. Rosco had picked up the crib and mattress. She needed to get home. She ran a list of possibilities to cook for supper for the two of them. Her stride lengthened as she neared her office again.

11

Emma picked up a pizza on the way home. Half pepperoni and half everything, not being sure what kind Rosco would like best. She listened for the kettle, needing a cup of chamomile tea to help calm her nerves.

She stared at the room where the crib would go. Afraid the social worker would look in the closet, she'd piled everything into her bedroom, including all her seasonal clothes, her decorations, and even her beloved collection of scarves.

A knock came on the door at the same time the kettle whistled. Emma rushed to grab the kettle off the stove and hurry to the door. She glanced down at her blouse, thinking she should have changed but had no time before opening the door.

Expecting Rosco, her enthusiasm fell at the sight of three women at her door. They held bags with pastel tissue paper and food.

"Surprise!" The one with short dark hair grinned. "I'm Holly, and this is Judy and Marge. Haden's helping Rosco get the crib from the truck. Can we come in?"

"Oh my." Emma's hand went straight to her heart. She leaned to the side, spotting two men with vests over their jackets and the Thunder Valley Christian Motorcycle Club patch.

"Rosco told her we were coming, right?" the one with curly salt-and-pepper hair asked.

"No. It's a surprise," the other older woman said louder in the woman's ear.

"Marge has trouble sometimes in her left ear. May we come in? We brought subs, and I ordered some pizzas."

"You're expecting more?" Emma glanced around. Rosco waved as he and another man carried a large box in her direction.

"Of course. The more, the merrier," Holly said brightly.

Emma glanced at the women and stepped back.

"Excuse us, ladies," Rosco said, turning his back to them and coming through the door. Emma stepped back, holding the door. After the men, the women entered.

"Where do you want it?" Rosco asked.

"Up the stairs to your right," she pointed, trying to think for a moment if she'd closed her bedroom door or had anything embarrassing lying around.

"I hope you don't mind. Rosco called us and asked us to help. We're from the Thunder Valley chapter of the Christian Motorcycle Club." Marge patted Emma's arm.

"Where should we put the food?" Judy asked.

"Um. In the kitchen. Straight back," Emma said, going to close the door.

"Wait!" a woman called, hurrying toward her door. Another car pulled up, and two others got out. "Don't forget us!"

Emma stood at the door, watching as three more women gathered boxes and bags in their arms. Behind her, the man with Rosco slipped past.

Rosco stood beside her. "My sister, Nicole, doesn't like being called Nicky, and the blonde one is my sister-in-law

Carrie. The one with the box in her hands is Jen, my brother Lucas's girlfriend."

"You invited all these people to my house?" she asked.

Rosco leaned in close, and she inhaled his masculine scent. Holding onto the door, she tried not to fall back into him. He pressed closer. "I knew how anxious you were, and it'll give Haden good practice for when he and Holly get married and have kids. My sister Nicole has kids, so she knows how to set up a nursery, and Holly is good with parties. I've got you covered."

He slid around her, pecked her on the cheek, and her hand went up to the spot.

"Slipped one in on you, did he?" the woman teased. She had to be Rosco's sister. The dark hair and the eyes matched. She had an armload of bags, and the blonde behind her laughed.

"We might have gotten carried away, but it's hard not to shower a baby with gifts, you know?" Carrie, or was it Jen, said.

Emma shook her head, figuring by the end of the evening she'd remember a few of their names.

She let them in and watched as Holly coordinated the food in the kitchen and Nicole instructed the men to get the crib set up. Jen and Marge folded clothes and stacked them, and they'd brought a hamper filled with yellow checkered baby bedding.

"I bought a blanket," Emma murmured as Holly handed her a cup of tea.

"It's okay. You're overwhelmed. Sit, have tea. I saw you had a pizza here, so I put it out with the subs. The rest should arrive any moment."

Emma sank onto her couch, amazed by the surrounding women.

"We've been praying for you and your family." Judy sat

beside her. "Do you have a picture? I'd love to see baby pictures."

Emma pulled out her phone, flipped until she came to one of the few she had of Isaac. A nurse had taken the best shot, one where she held Isaac, and Rosco sat beside her. They looked like a family, and it made her chest heavy. She let Judy fuss over the photo and held her cup of tea.

"So precious," Judy said, handing the phone to Marge, who passed it to Carrie, and soon all the ladies had seen the photo of her and Rosco and Isaac.

Twenty minutes later, more pizzas arrived, and two ladies Nicole called from her church brought diapers and a baby swing.

The women gathered around her little table in the kitchen, eating and sharing stories. Those who had kids shared wisdom and warning, and Emma listened. Her chest filled with an uncomfortable burn. She went into the kitchen to refill her tea.

"I'm taking the guys up some pizza while they work. Do you want to help?" Holly held out a plate she'd made for one of the guys.

"Sure." Emma followed, each step slower than the last. Holly pulled a can of soda from under her arm and held out the plate and drink to Haden. He leaned in, kissed Holly, and took the plate.

Rosco sat on the floor inside her spare room, screwing a bolt in the side of the crib frame. She crouched down, setting the plate beside him. "I forgot to grab you a drink. I can go back down and get you one."

"I've got it." Holly handed it over. She stood with Haden's arm around her waist.

"Thanks." Rosco took the drink.

Emma went to straighten when he caught her hand with his free one. Little zings of warmth wrapped around her palm. "What do you think?"

She found it hard to think around him. Emma stared at Rosco when he gave her a thousand-watt smile. "That good, huh?"

"Oh. No." She shook her head. "Wait. I mean."

Gah! He'd flustered her. How could she let him fluster her like this? Finally, she looked at the crib, partially finished, and the tension eased. "It's perfect."

"I don't know about perfect. I wouldn't put a kid in it until all the screws are in place and the mattress is inside," Haden said.

For a moment, Emma had forgotten about Haden and Holly in the room. She rose away from Rosco and brushed her hands down her hips. "Yes, well, that."

Holly laughed. "Stop. You're embarrassing her."

"What?" Haden stuffed a piece of pizza in his mouth.

Holly grabbed Emma. "Come on, let these men finish their task. Otherwise, we'll be here all night."

"I'm okay with that." Rosco winked, and Holly rolled her eyes.

Outside the room, Holly kept her arm around Emma's. "He's cute, isn't he?"

"Haden?" Emma asked.

Holly giggled. "I meant Rosco, but Haden's cute too. Otherwise, I wouldn't marry him."

"I thought you were marrying him because the two of you have always been in love with each other," Judy said, catching their conversation as they came back into the living room.

"There is that." Holly released Emma. "But I was referring to the way Rosco is like everyone's big brother trying to take care of us all."

Nicole plucked a potato chip out of a bowl on the table. "I hate to say this, but there isn't anything brotherly about my *little* brother's intentions toward you, Emma."

"Nope." Jen sat down in a chair and grabbed another hunk of turkey sub from a plate. "It's all for that baby."

Nicole gave Jen a look, and the girl stuffed her face with the turkey sub.

"Oh please." Carrie stacked the last of the baby clothes she stood folding. "He likes you. A lot."

Oh boy, was Emma in trouble.

For the next hour, the women carried clothes and toys and bedding upstairs. One woman from Rosco and Nicole's church brought a framed Mother's Prayer to hang in the room. Nearly after ten, the group filtered out, leaving Emma standing in a nursery ready for baby Isaac to come home.

Rosco lingered as she said her hundredth thank-you to Holly and Haden. He slipped his arm around her waist and it felt right. She barely knew the man, and he'd done so much for her and Isaac.

Oh Audra. Her heart ached. *Where have you gone? Please, Lord, keep her safe.*

"Those must be some heavy thoughts. Mind sharing?" Rosco asked.

"I was thinking of Audra. Thinking if she ever planned to keep Isaac or would she have dropped him off with his father and took off as our mother did."

"I'm sorry, Emma. I hadn't realized your mother didn't raise you."

"I'm glad she didn't." Deb wasn't the motherly type. She went to the kitchen. The ladies had all cleaned up before they left. There was nothing for her to do.

"Come on, let's sit on the couch."

"Don't you have to go? Isn't it getting late? I thought your bedtime was nine."

"I took a nap earlier today, so I could stay up to spend time with you."

He had a way with words. She'd give him that much.

Emma allowed him to lead her to the couch and sat beside him. He pulled her into his arms. "Thank you for today."

"*You* are thanking *me*? I should be the one thanking you."

She took his hand in hers, entwining their fingers. "No one has ever done something like this before for me."

"What, no parties?"

She shook her head, focusing on their fingers intwined. "No boyfriends. No parties. No mother, but I graduated seventh in my class, and I finished law school."

"You're amazing, do you know that?"

Emma looked up, and Rosco cupped her cheek. His thumb brushed right below her eye.

"I don't know what I would do without your friendship," she said.

Rosco's hand stilled. "I have to go."

"We just sat down." She dropped her gaze to his other hand, still holding hers.

"I know, but if we stay like this for much longer, I'll want to do more than sit by you." His tone sounded irritated, and he frowned as he pulled her hand from his, cupped the other side of her cheek, and tilted up her face. "Good night, Emma."

"You'll text me, so I know you made it home, okay?" She sounded like her father, but Emma felt his smile against her head. "Sure."

He kissed her on the forehead, leaving her on the couch as he showed himself out the door.

She pulled a pillow over from the couch, still warm from where his back had leaned against it. She rested her cheek there and closed her eyes, knowing he locked the door on the way out—her thoughts in turmoil.

12

Rosco lifted his hand to knock on Emma's door. He'd been standing on her porch for twenty minutes rehearsing in his head what to say when she opened the door.

Last night, his friends had all stepped up when he called and asked for help. It felt good knowing the club members, his family, and his church all had his back.

He wanted Emma to know he had her back. She needed someone, and he wouldn't let her do this alone.

Emma was getting under his skin, invaded his thoughts, and he knew better than to get too attached.

Last night, there on the couch, he should have never asked her to sit with him. All good relationships started with friendship, so why when Emma said that word did it sour Rosco's mood?

The door opened, and Rosco tried to remember if he'd knocked. Their gazes met in a torrent of blue, blending and separating in a mist of gray.

"What are you doing here?"

He lowered his hand, shoved it in his coat pocket. He'd rehearsed this but muttered it fast before he lost the nerve. He should have asked instead of pressing his luck. This morning,

Rosco almost forgot to turn twice during his route and would have missed two rows of houses if not for Melvin keeping an eye out.

"Has the social worker got here yet?"

Tilting her head, she looked at him with deep grooves forming at the side of her mouth. "No."

"Then I'm on time. Are you going to invite me in?" Before he lost his nerve.

She wore a pair of jeans and an oversized cable-knit sweater. She'd pinned her hair back with a barrette, and behind her, the house smelled of blueberry and coffee.

"I'm expecting Janet, the social worker, any moment."

"Listen, I can leave. I just wanted to come and show my support. I know how important this is to you. I've been thinking about you and this all morning." He couldn't get her or little Isaac off his mind. More so her, and it sent an odd sensation surging through him.

He liked her. More than liked her, and it frightened him half out of his wits. Especially since he had been down this road before. She'd like him, but as a friend, and he couldn't risk going through another 'let's just be friends' speech.

"I don't know how it would look, with the social worker and all." She glanced past him.

"We're about to find out, aren't we?" Emma could frown all she wanted. It wouldn't change them both standing there on the porch while a woman with a purple scarf got out of her car and walked their way.

"Good afternoon," the woman called. "I hope this is a good time."

Rosco stepped back, determined not to let Emma push him away. He wanted her to know he wasn't going anywhere. Friend or no friend, he would support her.

Without further discussion, Emma invited the social worker inside. He stepped in after her, staying in the front entrance. Emma shot him a few disparaging looks while she invited the social worker in for coffee and muffins.

"I'm Janet Summers."

"Rosco Reynolds."

"You found the baby."

"I did," Rosco said.

"I think we can skip the coffee and muffins until later. Would you like to see the room?" Emma asked.

As they headed upstairs, Emma told Rosco to help himself. Instead, he unlaced his muddy boots and followed the ladies upstairs.

Curious, he hoped to hear and see the social worker's reaction to the room they'd put together for the baby. Truth be known, he wished Isaac belonged to him and Emma. He wanted Audra safe and to return for Emma's sake. His sisters drove him crazy, but they were always there when he needed them. Last night had proved it.

"You've done a great job with the room," Janet said, writing some notes on her iPad.

She asked Emma some questions about her work schedule. "And do you have a daycare arranged, or do you plan on having someone else care for the baby while you work? I'll need to know, as it's important to ensure the care of the child."

Emma stammered. "I—well, I—" Rosco stepped in beside her, placed his hand on her back. "My sister-in-law Carrie will watch him in the mornings, and I'll take him in the afternoons until Emma gets off work."

"You have experience with children?" Janet asked.

"I've handled my fair share of diapers with my nephews and nieces," Rosco said.

Emma's lips parted, her eyes wide and staring at him.

"Are you two together?" Janet pointed her question at Emma.

They both said at the same time:

"No."

"Yes."

Janet's thin brows rose. "Which is it?"

"We're friends," Emma blurted. "Rosco's a good friend. He's helping me out, just until I find a daycare that can take Isaac when he's old enough."

Rosco dropped his hand from Emma. He allowed the two ladies to head downstairs while he lingered. He peered into the nursery at the crib. Solid and reliable. He and Haden made sure the baby's bed would hold up. Just like Rosco. Always there. Always reliable. Good. Solid, but never more than friends.

How could he make Emma give him a chance? And what would happen once Isaac came home? When they found her sister?

Down the stairs, he paused on the other side of the door.

"I feel it's important to let you know I've been to your mother's home this morning. She also wants to take in the child."

"Deb? She knows about Isaac?" Emma sounded perplexed.

Rosco ducked his head, not wanting to eavesdrop.

"As the grandparent, she has the right," Janet said.

"I'm not worried." Emma clutched the sides of her sweater. "I'm sure once you run your background checks, you'll see my mother has been in and out of rehabs because of her drug and alcohol addictions."

Their voices moved away, and Rosco went to the doorway, watching Emma walk Janet to the door.

She waved at him, and he lifted his hand, being polite.

Emma kicked at the leaves on the walk. He met her half-way. "Emma."

She shook her head, biting her lip.

He pulled her into his arms. Tense, he could feel she

wanted to scream. "I'm here. Tell me what you need me to do."

Anything to make her feel better.

"Rosco." She relaxed, resting her cheek against his leather jacket. He slipped his arms around her, feeling her shoulders slump. For half a second, he toyed with the idea of going after the social worker. He'd convince her Emma was the best option for Isaac. But the idea went as quickly as it came. He knew it wouldn't make a difference.

"It's going to be okay." For now, he would have to settle for being a good friend, the knowledge not settling well inside him as patience was never one of his strongholds.

She shivered in his arms.

"Let's get you inside. It's damp, and I have a feeling it will rain soon."

She muttered something against his coat. He leaned back, and she repeated it. "I have to go see Deb."

"Deb is your mother?"

She nodded.

Rosco pulled her in tighter, wanting to shield her from the cold and prolong their time together a moment longer.

Pressing her hand against his chest, she pushed back and put on a wobbly smile. "Thank you for coming. I need to go."

"Emma, you don't have to do this alone. It's why I'm here." What else could he say to make her see she could trust him, rely on him?

"If I take you to see Deb, she might get the wrong idea."

He held her hand against his heart. "Would that be so bad?"

He wouldn't push her, although her reluctance wounded him. He realized more than ever he wanted to meet her family. Usually, when a girl brought him home to meet her family, it never lasted long. The parents loved him, a good Christian guy who made a good living. But girls lacked interest in taking their relationship beyond friendship.

"You'll see when you meet her."

Okay, so maybe there was hope for him, for them, after all.

He waited while she grabbed a jacket and her bag. He didn't argue when she insisted on taking her car, and he didn't complain about the country music bellowing from the speakers. He hadn't pegged her for a country music girl.

They drove across town and pulled up alongside the street in front of one of the many row houses.

Emma glanced out her window to the house in direct view. Her knuckles turned white around the steering wheel.

"I never come here. Usually, Deb calls me when she wants something."

Rosco settled back in the seat, knowing from experience with women he'd best listen.

"She never wanted us. Not me. Not Audra. Not at least until we were older, and she figured we could be of use to her. She would show up at the house and argue with my father. I'd hear them from my room. He'd give her money. Then she'd go on her way. She didn't even care if she saw me. It's always about the money, about getting that next hit or that next drink. Audra's father was no better. He's a drunk she found in the bar. Except he had a wife."

"I bet that went over really well," Rosco muttered, reaching over and placing his hand on her knee.

"When Audra was twelve, she went to live with Deb. Her father went to jail, and his current wife wanted nothing to do with her, so she went to live with our mother. Deb tried to sell Audra to my father."

Rosco remained speechless.

"Yeah." Her lips pressed together, thinned.

"Your father is a terrific guy. I hope one day you'll invite me to meet him."

She glanced back out the window. "He didn't buy her. I mean, he didn't take Audra into our home. He told Deb to clean up and be a mother for once in her life. She'd use Audra as an excuse to dump her on the weekends for *sleepovers*. She'd disappear for weeks, sometimes months, with some guy she met. I often wondered if there were more of us. Kids."

The air between them thickened in the car. Outside, a mist fell across the windshield and gathered. A stream of moisture ran in little lines down the glass of the driver side window.

"That's why you became a family lawyer? You're doing a good thing. Here. For your clients. For your sister. Isaac." He squeezed her knee.

She blinked. "Danvers called me in his office yesterday. One of my clients doesn't think I'm giving enough attention to their case. I never wanted to take that case. Sometimes I hate the system. It breaks my heart."

And he could see her heart there on her sleeve.

"If I've gotten to know anything about you, Emma Harris, it is that you'll fight for what is right. Your heart is in the right place. Even I can see that in the little time since we met."

She nodded, biting her lip.

"We don't have to do this today." Or any other day, but he'd keep that to himself.

"My father said I should call her. I've been putting it off. Whatever her reasons for wanting Isaac, they're not good."

"You're afraid she has a chance to take him?"

She turned her head, her eyes a deep blue with flecks of gold beneath her lashes. Her face hardened as she said, "Not a chance. Once Janet runs a background check, she'll see Deb is unfit. It won't stop Deb from trying, especially if she thinks she can gain something from it."

"Then why are we here?" Rosco asked.

"To find out what Deb means to gain. Audra could have contacted her, and it's not enough for me to know she's alive. I need to know where she is. It's not fair to me, and it's not fair to that baby fighting for his life in that NICU ward."

"Alright, then. Let's go see Deb." Rosco reached for the handle of his door when Emma grabbed his arm.

"Wait. On second thought, stay in the car. I don't know what I was thinking. I shouldn't have dragged you along. It isn't your problem."

Rosco removed her hand from his arm. "It became my business the moment I found that baby in the trash. I wouldn't be here if I didn't want to be involved, and I wouldn't be here if I didn't care. About. You."

Emma blinked, looked away, and got out of the car. Rosco followed, glancing around the run-down neighborhood. Lifting his gaze to the gray sky overhead, he hoped for the rain to hold off.

13

You can do this, Emma. Don't let her intimidate you. She let anger fuel her motivation. It took several knocks and Emma pounding harder each time for Deb to come to the door. She opened it as far as the chain would allow.

The crow's feet by her eyes stretched out as her eyes narrowed. "What's this?"

"May we come in?"

Deb glanced at Rosco standing behind Emma. "Got yourself a man, huh?"

She closed the door. They heard the chain slide and the door open a moment later.

Dressed in floral leggings and a knotted tunic, Deb's painted eyebrows went straight to her dyed hairline. She'd gotten a cut and curl recently.

"Your father kick you out?" Deb leaned in the doorway.

Deb eyed Rosco, traveling from his head down to his black laced boots. It made Emma uncomfortable how her mother's gaze fixated on his waist, chest, and then his arms.

Rosco cleared his throat. "Mind if we step inside out of the damp weather?"

"I always expected you'd date a suit," Deb said.

"My family owns a trash disposal company." Rosco lifted his chin, his tone reserved.

"And here I thought one of Audra's biker friends had come back knocking on my door. Imagine my surprise. Never thought I'd see you here or bring a man with you. Your sister hook you up?"

"No," Emma said.

Deb stepped back. "Better get inside. Emma doesn't know what it's like to be cold."

Emma stepped inside far enough to give Rosco space and for Deb to shut the door. She ignored her mother's attempt to get a rise out of her.

Inside the small row house, the furniture was sparse. Someone had vacuumed the carpets as she could see the rug's lines from the yarns going the wrong way. It smelled of Febreze and cigarette smoke, the ceiling yellowed and spots of stains in the back corner of the wall.

"You going to introduce me or what?" Debra moved to a table near the door, drew out a cigarette from a pouch.

"Rosco, this is my birth mother, Debra. Deb, this is my friend, Rosco."

"Friend?" Debra lit her cigarette and laughed, smoke blowing out her nose. "Honey, I've had a lot of guy friends in my time, and none of them as good looking as this one."

Rosco coughed, and his neck turned a little red. Emma bit her tongue, reminding herself why they'd come here.

"We didn't come here on a social call," Emma said.

"You've always been like James, always to the point. She might have gotten her brains from her father, but the looks she got from me," Deb said to Rosco.

"I know the social worker was at your house this morning."

"Do you, now? Is that the lawyer talkin' in you, or is it because you're afraid I'll get the baby and you won't have any say in the matter what happens to the little tyke?" Deb took a long draw off her cigarette and let out the smoke slowly, pointing the stream away from Emma.

"Did you know Audra was pregnant?" Emma demanded, her emotions getting the best of her.

Deb hitched a hand on her hip and took a puff of her cigarette. "Imagine my surprise when the police came knocking on my door. Said Audra ran off, and they found the baby."

Deb's tone bothered Emma.

"You've been to the hospital to see him?"

"Well, yeah. Of course, the nurses won't let me hold him. Imagine having to see your grandbaby through the glass. They said he was born too early, didn't even think he'd make it."

Emma reached up and pinched her nose. "You're not on the list of visitors."

"Well, I am now." Deb stuck the cigarette back in her mouth.

It struck a chord with Emma. Since when did Deb play the concerned mother, let alone grandmother?

"You didn't think you could keep me from seeing my grandchild, did you?"

"No."

"A decent person would have called and told me. Instead, I had to hear it from the police." Deb crossed her arms, glaring at Emma.

Not at all intimidated, Emma held onto her purse strap. The heat radiating from Rosco at her back kept her focused. "You should pay your phone bill, then perhaps it would ring, and someone could get a hold of you."

"You know where I live. You're here, aren't you?"

Emma crossed her arms. Inside her head, she counted to ten and practiced her technique for staying calm around her mother.

"I knew my girl was in the family way. Mothers know these kinds of things. Especially when their girls come around to see them." Deb lowered her hand. "You in the family way? You get my girl in trouble?" Deb pointed at Rosco.

Rosco tensed behind her. "No, ma'am."

"I'm not the one we should be concerned with here." Emma ground the back of her teeth.

Deb held up her cigarette again. "That's right, Emma's too much of a good girl to get in trouble. Her father raised her right. Took her to church every Sunday."

It felt odd coming from Deb.

"When is the last time you heard from Audra?" Emma asked.

Debra tilted her head. She hadn't invited them to come in any further.

"She calls home, comes by, more than you," Deb said.

Rosco shifted his weight behind her. She appreciated his silent support.

"You two getting hitched?"

"It's not like that." Emma tucked back a strand of damp hair.

"Shame," Deb said.

"I need to know if you've heard from Audra," Emma pressed.

"The police are looking for her. It's all my fault," Deb said, her hand shook as she took another puff.

"How so?" Rosco interjected.

"I did this. She must be scared. So scared." Deb pressed the heel of her hand to her eye while holding the cigarette.

Rosco's hand landed on Emma's shoulder. She waited to see how Deb would play this out. When Emma remained quiet, Deb sniffled. "She call you?"

"Yes," Emma said.

"You wouldn't help her, would you?" Deb swore under her breath. Emma peeked a glance sideways at Rosco.

"I can't help her. She'll have to face the consequences of

abandoning her baby. I think Audra's in trouble, and I think you know where she is."

"I ain't telling you. Not if I did." Deb paced over toward the living area and back. "You'll give that baby to another family to raise." Deb's hand shook as she lifted the burning cigarette toward her lips. Ash fell to the dark brown carpet.

"He deserves a family who will care for him and take care of his needs." Emma ignored the questioning look on Rosco's face.

"He made you hard. I tried to take you back when I realized my mistake, but he had money, and I didn't."

"All you ever came for was the money." Emma refused to go to the past. Her mother's version would always differ from her memories. Things she wanted to leave behind, things she promised God she would forgive but couldn't forget.

Deb would forever try to use them to gain her will.

"I deserved to have a life," Deb's voice rose, and Rosco stepped up beside Emma. His fingers put pressure on her shoulder for her to step back. She lifted her hand and put it over his.

Emma brought the conversation back to their purpose of being there. "And so does Audra's baby. We both know the last thing you need in your life is a baby, so what is it you're really after? Do you think Audra will come back and live with you if you have the baby?"

Deb's hand went to her chest, smoke drifting from the end of her cigarette. "That baby is my grandchild. She'll need help. It's hard being a single mother, and they don't allow babies in those college apartments. I checked."

"How many months back on the rent are you this time?" Emma asked.

"See how she talks to her mother?" Deb addressed Rosco standing behind Emma.

Deb waved her hand with the cigarette. "So what if I get

money on the side for watching the kid? I got bills, and Audra's going to need a place to stay."

"I should have known." Emma's hand slipped away from Rosco's.

"You got no right to judge me. Coming into my house and acting all high and mighty. I know you think you're better than me. Big shot attorney. Got an education. Everything you ever needed because of me, and what thanks do I get?"

"You?" Emma sucked in a breath.

"I knew your father would take far better care of you than I ever could." Deb's gaze fell to the floor.

Oh please, Emma took another settling breath. *Here we go with the pity act.* Rosco stood behind her, his hands at his side, his face neutral in all this. What he must think... Emma should have taken the time to prepare him. Instead, she'd blurted out and spilled all her insecurities in the car to a man she'd known for less than a week. Okay, maybe a week today, but too short a time to dump her issues on him.

If Deb didn't scare him away, she didn't know what else would. She reached back, and his hand connected with hers. It grounded her. How could she ever think not to have him in her life?

"And you think you're a good fit to take care of Audra's baby?" Emma said.

"Just until she comes back, and she'll come back. She's just scared. You don't know what it's like. I know what it's like." Deb took another puff of her cigarette. "You know your father never even offered to marry me, and he called himself a Christian." She made a noise deep in her throat. "Now Audra's daddy, we had an understanding. Tell them how it is right up front!" She pointed at Rosco.

"How many times have you gone to the hospital?"

"Which one?" Deb asked.

So, her mother had been in a few hospitals lately. She wore too much makeup to see the actual shade of her skin.

"Where the baby is."

Deb shrugged. "Like I told the social worker that was here this morning, I got things to get ready. Tilly across the road said I could have the crib her daughter left last month when her old man took her back. I had to pay a kid twenty dollars to bring it over here. And that whole business of foster care requiring paperwork for your flesh and blood is ridiculous. That's my grandbaby. It's not going anywhere else but right here with me until Audra comes back."

Emma didn't bother correcting Deb. Isaac was a *he*, not an *it*. This made Emma wonder if Deb even knew the gender of her grandchild.

"You applied to be a foster parent?" Foster parents received a monthly stipend from the government for taking in children.

Deb took a step to the side, smashed the little remaining of her cigarette into the ashtray. "Might as well. They don't pay me enough as it is. A woman's got to live. Who knows when Audra will show. That old man of hers must be after her."

"You know who the baby's father is?" Rosco asked.

Deb smiled. "Sure do. Emma here isn't the only one who brought her man home to meet Momma."

Between the smoke and the stench of the closed-up house, Emma found it harder to breathe.

Rosco's hand landed on her back.

Emma's eyes watered. "You've met him."

"Did I just say I did?" Which translated to Deb wouldn't say if she did.

"His name?" Emma felt a headache coming on. It was a mistake coming here. Her mother would never change.

"Why don't you ask your boyfriend here? He knows him." Then Deb took a step closer, squinted. "Where's your vest? Your patch?"

Rosco motioned to open his leather jacket, when Emma

slapped her hand across his to stop him. "Do you know where Audra is?"

"What's the matter, Emma, you don't think I don't know a biker when I see one?"

Rosco grinned, and it sent those zings in her stomach as his dimples appeared. Distracted both by her mother's question and Rosco, she shook her head and remembered where this was going. "Audra?"

"How should I know?" Deb turned and plopped down in an old recliner.

"You're lying."

"Maybe." Deb looked straight at her. "We don't need you around here. I can take care of Audra and that baby. Take your biker boyfriend and go about your business. I have everything taken care of, so stay out of it."

"They won't give you custody of the child." Emma's body trembled. Rosco laid a hand on her shoulder. "Let's go."

Deb leaned forward. Her eyes narrowed. "You'd do that to me? You were always such an ungrateful child! You wouldn't have what you do if it wasn't for me! And your sister, you'd see her dead, wouldn't you?" Deb shouted.

"Dead?" Emma's insides went cold.

Deb's eyes filled with tears. "I need a drink." She flew up out of the chair and headed to the kitchen. "No." She stopped by the counter. "I told that woman I was clean. Gotta stay clean." Deb turned her head, pinning Emma with her stare. "That baby means more to me than it will ever mean to you. If you love your sister, you'll keep your nose out of this."

Deb moved around the counter, yanked the refrigerator door open. She swore under her breath and slammed the refrigerator door shut again. She started mumbling to herself, and Emma pulled out her phone.

"What are you doing?" Rosco said, his tone hushed.

"Evidence." She hit the record button. Then a few

moments later, Deb turned, her eyes wide and wild as she stalked toward them.

"Get out! Get out of my house and don't you come back!"

Rosco tugged on Emma and pulled her through the doorway. "It was nice to meet you."

"Get. Out." Deb snarled, slamming the door in their faces.

Emma stood, phone in hand, staring at the door.

"Come on, let's go."

The rain came down in a steady drizzle. Emma clung to her phone, frozen inside. Her numb fingers fumbled to find her keys when they got to the car. He took them from her, led her around to the passenger side. "I think it best if I drive."

She slipped down into the seat, dropping her purse at her feet and holding onto the phone. Once Rosco adjusted the seat and put the key in the ignition, he said, "Well, that went —well."

"You can see why I don't associate with her." Emma looked at the phone. A snapshot of her mother yelling, hair jutting out, and her hand swinging reflected back at her. "It's been a while since I've seen her that way."

"You handled it well." He drove them down the street.

"I'm sorry. I shouldn't have brought you here. I shouldn't have let you meet her this way." She kept her focus out the side of the window.

"I guess you'll just have to make it up to me by letting me meet your dad." Rosco's voice was light, teasing.

It brought a twitch to her lips. She peeked a glance at him. "You'd still want to meet the rest of my family after that? Aren't you afraid now?"

"I'm a big bad biker dude, remember? You can't scare me that easy." He grinned again, and it became contagious.

"She knows where Audra is. There is more than she'd tell us. She wouldn't go through all this trouble if she didn't think there was something in it for her."

"You mean the fostering?"

She watched houses go by, one by one.

"She's just doing it to get money. I can see if I can keep her from seeing Isaac at the hospital, but I don't know if I should. If she's really trying to be clean—" Emma's voice trailed off.

How many times had Deb gone to rehab with promises of cleaning up and staying clean?

"You have to believe she will."

"Oh, me of so little faith," she sighed. "I used to pray all the time for her to change. That God would help her stay clean, and when she came to see my dad, it would be because she wanted to see me, spend time with me, not dump off Audra or ask Dad for cash. She probably sold her television. That's why there wasn't one in the room."

"Some prayers take longer to answer than others," he said.

"Or some don't get answered at all."

"The key is not to give up." Rosco took Emma home. They watched a techno-thriller, and Rosco fell asleep on the couch. She pulled a blanket over him. Upstairs, a pile of casework lay on her bed. Her heart was not in it. She curled up beside him, her head on his chest, listening to the beat of his heart and the rain coming down harder outside.

Her finger scrolled on her phone, finding the pictures she had of Isaac. The one of her and Rosco. She lingered on the one of Audra. She'd snapped it from another photo she found at Audra's apartment. Divided by age and fathers, they shared the same round face. Audra's hair was darker, and she'd favored the blue streak. It showed her wild side, her defiance against an unfair world.

"I know you're alive, but please, Audra. Call," she whispered into the phone.

Rosco wiggled beside her, settling deeper into the cushions against her couch.

The key is not to give up.

14

At eight in the morning, Rosco pulled up in front of Emma's house.

She took one look at his long leather jacket and said, "You rode your bike?"

"You make it sound as if I jumped on a bicycle and pedaled the entire way out here."

She must have at least had a cup of tea, and he liked the way her cardigan hung open. An infinity sign peeked out of her rounded neckline from her necklace. She wore boots, and they looked good on her. Suitable for riding on the back of his motorcycle if he could convince her to take it for a spin. There wouldn't be many more days before the snow hit and his motorcycle got parked for a few months.

She'd been adamant last night when he'd invited her to breakfast with the club—no motorcycle.

Eventually, he'd talk her into it.

"Ready to go?" He'd told Haden to save them a spot if he and Emma got detained. They'd agreed for him to pick her up at eight, knowing they needed to get there by eight thirty. Depending on how long it took her to get ready, he hoped they would make it on time. She went inside to grab her purse.

"I'd like to stop by the hospital after. If you can drop me off, I'll get an Uber home."

"I'll go with you. I want to check on our little man." Since when had Isaac become theirs? He shouldn't think that way, but he did.

"Do you want to grab a jacket?"

She closed the door, checked the knob to make sure it was locked. Down the street, a car pulled out of a driveway and went past them.

"It'll warm up later." She stepped off her porch, gazed down the street. The leaves and the grass glistened with moisture, and a nip in the air made him pull his leather jacket closed.

He turned the heat on in the truck on the way over. The cab stayed warm for her to get inside. He turned on the radio, and Christian rock blared. Quickly, he turned it down.

She buckled her seat belt and grinned. "So where are we going again?"

"Denny's. I hope you like eggs."

She scrunched up her nose. "Ew."

"You don't like eggs?"

"Is that a problem?" she asked.

"Not for me." He reached over and took her hand.

"No eggs or just omelet eggs?"

"The kind I can taste."

Soon, he pulled into Denny's parking lot. She got a text, and he walked around to open her door. She hesitated, reading the message, then got out of the truck. "Thanks."

His eyes lowered to her mouth, and he stepped in close. Emma slipped around him, phone in hand. He hung his head and closed the door. Perhaps he hadn't read her right.

Distracted, she headed toward the diner. Rosco held open the door. Inside, Haden and Holly had saved their seats.

"Everyone, this is Emma," he introduced her.

Emma put away her phone. She smiled at the other club members.

"We've met. I'm Judy."

"And I'm Marge."

"I remember," Emma said.

Rosco pulled out a seat for her across from Holly and took the one beside Emma across from Haden.

Larry and Steve and several of the other club members leaned in, deep in discussion over coordinating the next run to claim the revolving trophy between the organization's chapters.

"What can I get you?" A blonde with her hair pulled back in a twist came up next to Rosco.

"Coffee and a stack of pancakes."

"And you, hon?" the blonde asked Emma.

"Tea, and I'll have a waffle please, with strawberries."

"Since when do you only eat pancakes?" asked Haden.

"Since Emma doesn't eat eggs," Rosco said.

"Any news on your sister, dear?" Judy asked.

Emma shook her head.

"We'll keep praying." Judy reached over, placing her hand on Emma's. "It's hard, but we're all here for you and your family."

"I appreciate that." Emma pulled her hand back onto her lap, her gaze on the placemat.

Holly shared pictures with Judy of wedding things.

"Any news from our *friend?*" Rosco asked Haden.

"No. You?" Haden reached around Holly and rested his arm on the back of her chair.

Tempted to do the same, Rosco placed an elbow on the table as the waitress returned to pour him coffee and set Emma's tea in front of her.

Rosco shook his head.

While they waited for their breakfast, they listened to club news. Judy passed around the attendance sheet, and Marge made a note of Beast's absence for the past few months.

"Charlie coming home soon?" Larry asked Holly. Her father was still recovering from the accident a couple of months ago.

"Before Christmas." Holly smacked Haden's hand as he reached for her bacon.

Emma kept her phone close to her silverware. Seeing her hand resting on it, Rosco leaned his shoulder into her. "You good?"

"I keep thinking any minute she'll call. I wake up sometimes at night thinking I heard my phone, but there are no new messages or calls."

"I'm sorry."

The waitress brought their breakfasts.

"I guess I hoped after visiting Deb yesterday maybe Audra would reach out."

"Oh." Holly almost spilled her coffee. "How did yesterday go?"

Emma picked up a strawberry, dipped it in whipped cream atop her waffle. "The social worker was pleased with the room."

"I detect a *but?*" Judy couldn't help overhearing, sitting this close to them.

"She was concerned about my job, and it seems my mother has expressed interest in being Isaac's guardian."

"That's good, right?" Judy asked.

Rosco shook his head. Judy hurried and stuffed a bite of eggs in her mouth.

"My mother didn't raise my sister or me," Emma said.

Halfway through eating his pancakes Emma's phone rang. With all the noise in the diner, she scooted her chair away from the table.

Rosco kept his eyes on her, half listening to Marge read the letter sent from one of the local churches asking them to take part in their annual Christmas donation drive.

Emma turned away, getting up and walking further from the table. Her shoulders pulled back, and her hair streamed down below her shoulders. She wore it down, with a touch of gloss on her lips and a touch of color above her eyes.

Yesterday, he'd woken almost around supper and found her at the kitchen table. He made a lousy date and vowed he would do better.

Folders and papers lay scattered around her, and a pair of reading glasses perched on her nose. Rosco remembered her curling up against him, the smell of coconut in her hair.

She'd covered him with a fuzzy blanket and pulled off his boots.

It rained through the night, and he'd stayed past ten. Pulling up to his place above Reynold's Disposal, he'd glimpsed a shadow near the large garage doors.

He'd waited, watched until the rain slowed and the outside lights stopped playing tricks on him. Still, he couldn't shake the feeling someone had followed him. It took three chapters of a fantasy novel to get his mind to settle. Even then, thoughts of Emma lingered in the back of his mind.

Her head bowed, and Rosco rose.

"Everything okay?" Haden looked across the table at him.

"I'll find out." Rosco moved around the waitress refilling coffee further down the table. Emma drifted to the front of the diner, near the windows.

"Okay." Her eyes, glazed over and wide, met his.

"What's wrong?" Instantly, he went on alert. She shook her head, listening.

"I'm on my way." Her eyes searched his, silently asking him permission to take her wherever she needed to go.

"Emma." He kept his tone low.

Pulling the phone from her ear, she said, "Isaac. We need to get to the hospital."

"Grab your purse. I'll take care of the bill."

He moved to the counter, asked for the check. The manager waved down the waitress. "Sorry, but we need to hurry."

Emma grabbed her purse from the back of her chair. Holly got up and followed. "Is everything okay?"

"The hospital called. I can't stay. We need to go." Emma moved closer to the door.

Holly took her hands. "Whatever it is, we'll be praying for you. If you need anything, you have Rosco call."

"Thank you." Emma hugged Holly. The two women murmured something. The waitress finished ringing up the check, and Rosco gave her a sizable tip. He had his road clothes on, even though he'd failed to convince Emma to embrace her wild side and climb aboard his bike.

Haden met him halfway to Emma. "Everything okay?"

"It's Isaac. They have to go." Holly filled him as Emma took Rosco's hand. Outside, he helped her into this truck.

Silence rode along with them on the way to the hospital.

———

"I'm sorry, but you will not be able to go in and see him. You'll have to stay on this side of the glass until the infection is healed."

"Infection?" Emma asked.

"Bacterial infection. I'm afraid it's spread into his lungs. He's intubated, so he's breathing, but it will take time for the antibiotics to run their course. Since he's premature, you understand the risks to his immune system at this stage," the doctor explained.

"How could this have happened?" Rosco asked.

"It could have come from an outside source. Someone who visited him that wasn't feeling well. It's hard to say."

"We're the only ones who have been to see him. What if

by holding him…" Emma couldn't finish her sentence, her throat was closing.

"You washed your hands. We donned the gowns." He slipped his fingers between hers.

"I wish I could give you the answers you want, but I don't know. We're doing all we can. Let's give the antibiotics time to work. Until then, I'm going to have to insist no one but my staff handles him. It's important to keep him in a sterile environment until he has a chance to build his immune system."

Emma leaned away, her gaze roaming the doctor's face, searching for what he wasn't saying to her.

Rosco thanked the doctor, allowing her to move away, free her hand to press it against the glass. Her forehead leaned against the cool surface.

Her first thoughts were to call someone. Her father? But her eyes found Rosco, his gaze intent on little Isaac in his incubator. A machine near the end, with tubes going down. They'd placed a tube down Isaac's throat, and the sight nearly undid her.

"My mom always says it gets worse before it gets better."

She drew in an unsteady breath. Rosco stood behind her and placed his hands on her shoulders. "Things like this happen. He's a fighter. It'll make him stronger."

It would delay bringing him home. Delay dealing with Deb. Give the police more time to find Audra and reunite them. If there was time…

She squeezed her eyes shut.

"Hey." Gently, he spun her around. "Nothing is going to happen to him. You hear me? Nothing."

"You don't know that." She stepped closer, his arms sliding down and going around her. She inhaled his warm, inviting scent, trying to absorb his strength, and for the first time in her life, she wanted to hold on to Rosco as more than a friend. He'd become much more than a friend—someone she cared for and could see their future in such little time. But a future without Isaac shook her to her core. She gasped to hold in the sob, but it spilled and released. She could do nothing but let out the emotions held in for so long. Rosco rocked her, held her through the storm of raging emotions.

Oh Lord, that baby. Please. He had to get better.

She buried her face against the leather, felt the slide of her tears against the slippery surface of her cheek.

She could blame her reaction on the reservoir she'd built over the years. Who would have known a baby, her sister's baby, could wring her out this much?

When she finally got a hold of herself, she stepped back and tried to wipe away the last evidence of her meltdown. Rosco brushed away the dampness with his fingers. Tilting her chin, he said, "I'm not going anywhere. I want you to know that. You're not alone, Emma. I'm here."

She caught her bottom lip in her teeth, speechless by his admission.

Rosco glanced down at her mouth, swallowed.

Raw from the emotions breaking free inside her, she nearly leaned in, pressed her tear-stained lips to his. She held back, studying him, the width of his nose, the tousle of his hair from where he ran his hands through it earlier. Every shade of brown and something darker made her itch to bury her fingers through the mass.

"Where's my grandbaby?" Deb's raspy voice caused Emma to still.

Emma found her voice. "What is she doing here?"

"Me?" Deb spotted her and marched up to her. "The hospital called me."

Emma closed her eyes, feeling dizzy from the over-whelming scent of cigarettes wafting from Deb, thankful Rosco held on, keeping her steady.

"They shouldn't have done that."

"I'm his next of kin," Deb's voice rose. A nurse walking down the hall paused.

"It's alright," Emma said to reassure the nurse, more than herself, that they'd get through this.

"So am I." Emma kept her voice low, controlled.

Deb moved to walk around her.

"You can't go in there," Rosco said.

Grateful for his support, Emma leaned into them. "No one can. He has a bacterial infection. They've had to intubate him."

"What's that mean?" Deb paled. Maybe she'd misjudged her mother's concern. After all these years, all those prayers?

A grim line pressed across Deb's lips. *Oh no, she was still the same.* She wouldn't let a second of shock cloud her assessment. Only she wished more than once she was wrong.

"It means we'll have to wait and pray the antibiotics heal the infection."

"No big deal." Deb waved her hand. "Babies get sick all the time. Here I thought he was dying."

"He's not out of the woods yet." Emma swiped at the last of the moisture running down her cheeks.

"He won't be going home anytime soon."

Deb went over to the glass, stood with her back to Emma. Silently, her mother stared into the room with all the other NICU babies.

"Better he stays. Get the care he needs," Deb said, more to herself than anyone.

Rosco gave Emma a little nudge, and she stepped up by the glass, looking ahead to the babies inside. Three, the one to the left, her nephew. A nurse walked around checking on them, glanced over, and smiled.

"Well, no sense standing around here watching them sleep. I got places to go and people to see,"

Her mother reached in her purse and pulled out a tissue, offering it to Emma.

Slowly, Emma took the tissue. Deb took another long look

at the baby, shook her head, and walked away, leaving Emma standing there, tissue in hand.

"She came," Rosco said.

"Yeah." Emma curled the tissue in her hand.

"Ever think about forgiving her?"

She had. A long time ago. Or at least she'd tried. Then her mother would do the same thing repeatedly, and she'd remember the pain of being left behind, unwanted. Of being used for what she had and not who she was—seven times seven.

"I've tried." And maybe trying wasn't good enough.

"Forgiving someone doesn't mean you have to invite them back into your life. That's your choice when you're ready. If you're ever ready."

"Have you ever needed to forgive someone?"

"Yeah." And that's all he said on the matter.

"And did you?" she asked.

"It wasn't easy, but my situation wasn't the same as yours."

She would have asked him more, but a nurse approached. They had visitors down the hall. Only family was allowed through the doors that led to the NICU.

Near the nurses' station, Haden and Holly met them.

A half hour later, Steve and Judy showed up. Half of Rosco's Christian motorcycle club came within the hour and formed a prayer circle around Emma.

Holly held onto her hand. "They did this when my father had his accident. I didn't understand it then, but now that I look back, I don't know what I would have done without their prayers to get us through it." Rosco held the other one, while Steve led them in prayer for baby Isaac, for Audra—and silently Emma included her mother, Deb.

15

Sebastian dumped an armload of parts onto the workbench in the back of the Sharks' chop shop. He pulled out his phone, hissing at the message. Stuffing the phone back in his pocket, he walked off.

"Hey! Where do you think you're going?" Puffer, a big dude, more belly than brawn, came marching Sebastian's way.

"Office. The big man wants to see me." Sebastian paid Puffer no attention.

The large man stopped short, jerked his chin up. "Don't forget you got more deliveries to make."

He'd made several deliveries today; luckily none of those were to his buddy Haden's shop. Soon, this would all come to a stop. He'd been stashing evidence in his saddlebags for the past several weeks.

"Beast!"

Tiger stepped into the shop.

Puffer's beady eyes landed on Sebastian. The man had spent time in prison and had more offenses than than Sebastian had walked the earth.

He tried not to cringe as Tiger waited for him. He said

nothing. Pike sent Tiger, which meant the boss man had gotten impatient. Not good.

"Pike's waiting."

"See me coming?" Sebastian walked past Tiger, the scar on Tiger's nose pale against his skin. Sebastian could feel Tiger's eyes boring into his back the entire walk to Pike's office.

He didn't have to bother knocking. Moray stood at the door. "He's waiting."

Sebastian ignored the snarl on Moray's lips. He kept his Glock tucked against his back, under his vest. Inside Pike's office, an older woman turned her head toward him. Her pale face and sagging flesh around her cheeks made her eyes sink in. Eyes that were bloodshot and wide assessed him.

He could smell the copper tang of blood in the room. "Come in, have a seat." Pike leaned back on the old vinyl executive chair.

A mist of smoke and something sweet drifted from behind him. Pike quirked a smile. For a second, Sebastian almost missed it.

"You wanted to see me?" Sebastian crossed his arms. No way would he sit down and let Pike trap him.

"You keeping things from me?" Pike leaned forward.

Sebastian shook his head.

Sitting in front of him, the woman's hands shook.

"Tell him what you told me." Pike leveled his gaze on the woman.

"Mind if I get her a drink first?" Sebastian glanced around Pike's office. He'd come in here before, slipping in at night, trying to case the place and find what he needed to close Pike permanently. Behind the president of Sharks, a navy bottle of Havana Club sat beside a tipped-over tumbler. To his right, a fridge stood, filled with soda. The man had a particular taste, liking his rum and Coke and drinking alone.

Sebastian had no taste for the stuff. He tilted his head to the side, glancing at the woman's hands again.

Pike's gaze followed Sebastian's, and the president gritted the back of his teeth. "Get her a drink."

"Something stiff. Not that watered-down stuff you gave me before," she demanded.

A few moments later, an alcoholic beverage dropped onto her lap. She flicked the tab and took a long drink.

"Better?" Piked asked.

The woman needed a rehab center, not another drink, but Sebastian couldn't say it out loud. For the past month, he'd worked to climb the ranks and get Pike to trust him. Another month and the gang would initiate him. He'd get his cut, and it would pull him deeper into his new identity as a member of the Sharks.

It made his stomach roll, watching the woman slurp her beer and her eyes go glassy. It took more than alcohol to put a shine in one's eyes. He'd seen it too many times in his days of pulling drunk and drugged-up drivers over on highway patrol.

"It's yours. I know it's yours. You'll pay me, right? That's the deal, or I'm not telling you which hospital." She burped.

Sebastian rolled his eyes. He crossed his arms, standing over to the side where he could see both the woman and Pike. Moray stayed by the door, and Tiger went out of sight. The door, a few feet to his left, closed. Sebastian knew Tiger stood outside it.

"What's this got to do with me?" Sebastian shifted his weight to the other foot. Who was this woman? Why did Pike have someone's mother in his office? The women he brought into his office rarely had gray streaks in their hair.

He liked them young and lively. It sent another sickening stir to his stomach. The more he looked at the woman—her sagging skin, her round face—he saw a slight resemblance.

"You're holding out on me," Pike said.

"I've done everything you've asked me to do."

Pike leaned back further and turned his attention to the woman.

"Dory had a kid," Pike said. He watched Sebastian for a reaction.

Sebastian swallowed, trying to remain calm.

"Ten grand and a thousand a month after." The woman clutched the can in her hands.

Pike ignored her outburst. "You knew about this?"

"I had my suspicions. I brought you the article in the paper about the dumpster baby."

Tugging on his beard, Pike leveled his stare on the woman. She shrank back in her seat. "I'll give you twenty grand if you tell me where she is."

The woman bit her lip, chewed on it. The hunger in her eyes made Sebastian step closer to her. "She's at the Super 8 on Solomon Run Road."

Pike stood, a broad smile going across his sinister face.

Sebastian's arms slipped from across his chest to his sides.

Pike looked past the woman. "Moray, see that Dory's mom gets what's coming to her."

Sebastian sucked in a breath.

Moray walked over, grabbed the older woman by the arm. "What about the baby? A thousand a month, and I'll take care of it for you."

Pike snorted. "As if the social worker will hand over a kid to the likes of you. I take care of my own, don't you worry."

Dory's mom yelped as Moray pulled her out of the office. Sebastian turned to follow. He needed to keep up with Moray, but Tiger stepped in his way as they headed down the hall, Dory's mom shouting, "Where you taking me? Where's my money?"

"Don't you worry about the money," Moray said. "I'll get it for you right after another drink."

Sebastian's skin chilled. He wanted to ram into Tiger and

run after Moray. Pike walked in front of the desk and cracked his knuckles.

"Don't ever trust a woman," Pike said.

Sebastian remained quiet. Pike liked to think he was a big fish around these parts, so he called his gang the Sharks. Twice Sebastian had risked his cover to help a woman. Could he risk it again?

He had no doubt Pike meant for Moray to take out Audra's mother. If he stayed here with Pike, he wouldn't get to her in time. If he went, Pike would confirm what he figured the Shark president already suspected.

He clenched his teeth together, hating this part of his job, hating the decision that weighed on him. The police force sent him into this operation alone, and he knew the risks.

"What will you do with her?"

"Her?" Pike pointed to the door. "She's nothing. The nerve of the hag to waltz in here thinking I'd give her money. Let alone I'd want her to raise some brat for me."

"How do you know she's telling the truth?" Sebastian asked.

"Desperate women do desperate things when they need their next hit," Pike said.

"She's lying. Did you see her eyes? She's a junkie," Sebastian tried to reason. Where was Moray taking her?

"You have a lot to learn. I like you, Beast. You've got a level head. You don't dive into the crap like the rest of my guys or go off half-cocked. I can use you around here. Consider yourself one of us." Pike moved to the fridge near his desk. Pulling out a Coke, he pulled back the tab, flipped over the glass, and poured it half full. Setting it down, he added rum. He held it out toward Sebastian, and Sebastian shook his head.

"We'll baptize you at Saturday night's meeting. You'll need a new name," Pike said, then took a drink.

"What is it you want me to do?" Sebastian knew enough to know Pike's offer came with a condition.

"You know about the brat. Not even those hammerheads figured out to pick up and read the paper. You're smart." Pike eyed him. "Which is why I want you to bring her to me."

Slowly, the chill gripped his chest.

"And the baby?"

"Chum says it's at Conemaugh Hospital in the premature ward. It probably won't make it." Pike took another sip of his drink. "I've got boys watching. If she's not at the motel like the old broad says, then sooner or later, Dory will show up for the kid. Either way, she's mine. You understand?"

"You want me to bring her to you. Here?"

"Yeah. You bring her here." Pike put down his drink. "Nobody better lay a hand on her, you get me? She's mine to take out."

"What about the kid?"

Pike slammed down his empty glass. "It leaves the hospital and we'll put it back in the trash where they found it. Tiger will go with you."

Bile rose in Sebastian's throat. Quickly he turned and marched away. Tiger was not far behind.

———

Sebastian waited until he found his opportunity to elude Pike's watchdog. He couldn't risk anyone overhearing him making a call or running straight for Audra. He worked in the common room, hung close to the pool tables among the patched brothers, and when Tiger became distracted with Cat, one of the club's ladies, he slipped out. Beast rode fast, ignoring the bite of the cold against his chest.

One thing he learned about Pike is the bastard took his time, like a predator hunting prey. He probably sent someone to verify the old woman's information first. A few of the regulars were out, but none had come back while Sebastian lingered.

Around one in the morning, Sebastian pulled his bike behind the motel and entered Audra's room.

He expected her to be asleep and used the special knock, and he was relieved when she slid off the chain to let him enter. Inside, the soft glow of the television lit the room.

A takeout bag lay crumpled on the table along with a pizza box. Sebastian slid the bag from his shoulder and sat it on a chair.

"You ordered out." He unzipped the bag.

"I got hungry. You haven't come in days."

"I told you I'd come when I could get away."

"It's just takeout. Not like anyone knows I'm here."

She settled on the edge of the bed, pulling a pillow against her and hugging it.

"I told you not to contact anyone." She'd left him no choice. Chief Razek had yelled for a good twenty minutes. At least he waited to make contact at a gas station while Tiger was inside taking care of business.

"I ordered takeout. I used the cash you left me." Audra huddled up on the bed.

"Maybe, but you called more than the pizza guy."

"I swear."

"Don't lie to me, Audra." Sebastian paced at the bottom of the bed. He raked his fingers through his hair. "I don't have time for this. Shaking Tiger wasn't easy, and I can't blow my cover."

"Tiger followed you?" Real fear wobbled in her voice.

Sebastian turned on his heel, wearing a path in the hotel carpet. "Pike assigned us to find you."

"You led him here?" She jumped off the bed. "I'm dead. I'm so dead."

"Yeah," he said. "We both are."

The terror on her face went straight to his bones.

"Please. Oh *pleeeease*. No." She paled, her knees buckling as she sat back down on the bed. Almost two weeks was not enough time to heal the bruises on her face or the wounds she hid beneath her clothes.

"I warned you."

"It was just my mother. Okay? I just wanted someone to know I was alive. My baby," her voice cracked, the tears spilled down her eyes.

Sebastian pulled the paper from the bag, tossed it on the bed beside her. "Read it."

He went over to the bedside table, clicked on the light.

"What's this?" She pulled the paper closer, looked at the headline.

He waited.

A few minutes later, she cried harder.

And still, he let her cry. She deserved time to let the reality of her situation sink in, and he'd have given her all the time they could spare. They needed to pack up and go.

"He's alive," she whispered, clutching the paper. "I have to go to the hospital."

"You're dead." Sebastian moved closer. He placed both his hands on her knees and crouched at her feet.

"Please. You have to take me to see my baby."

"Thanks to your mother, you take one step in that hospital, and Pike will not only find your son, but he'll get what he's been after. You."

She sucked in her breath, her head shaking. "How? My mother? What does she have to do with this?"

"She made a deal with Pike that involves your son. There's a bounty on your head, Audra. She went to collect."

Audra's eyes widened, and Sebastian's hands tightened on her legs. He should have ignored Razek, gotten her away sooner.

"She knew he was alive and didn't tell me. *You* knew, and…" She gulped, on the verge of a panic attack.

"The best thing you can do for your baby is to die, Audra." He swallowed down the foul taste in his mouth. He'd sworn to protect her.

"Die?" She kicked him and scrambled across the bed. "You are the liar! You work for Pike! You're a—" She pointed, her hand shook. "Dirty cop!"

Slowly, Sebastian rose. "I'm sorry, Audra. I can't keep you protected from Pike, not when your mother told him where you are for money. I told you not to call anyone or contact anyone. You told her where you are."

She blanched.

"You understand now the only way to keep you alive is for Audra Barnhart to die."

"You're going to hand me over to him."

"My contact has a new ID ready. We just have to get you moved to another place away from here."

A knock jolted them both.

Sebastian moved around the bed. Audra slid off it on the other side, backing away near the wall. She grabbed a lamp attached to the stand.

He held up his hand. "It's okay. I called in one of our detectives to take you to a safe house."

"And my baby?" Audra asked.

"Your sister is dealing with social services to ensure he gets the best care."

"She'll give him to a family. She'll let someone adopt him."

Another knock came to the door, this time with more force.

He moved to the door. "Don't you want him safe?"

Audra covered her mouth. Sebastian opened the door. In his haste, neither one had replaced the chain. As soon as the doorknob turned, the door shoved open, and Tiger stood with Puffer and Hammer behind him.

16

On the third night since Isaac went on the antibiotics, Emma spent the night at the hospital.

His responses had slowed, and they'd put in a feeding tube beside the one to his lungs.

He's a fighter. He's stronger than this. But sometime during the second day, she tried to prepare for the worst.

For once in her life, she couldn't ensure someone's safety. At home, she stood in the nursery in her room staring at the empty bed—a bed she hadn't prepared.

Rosco came every day after he ran his route with the garbage truck. The temperatures outside had dropped, and frost edged the windows of her office.

Lori fielded her calls, and she decided it was best not to take on any new cases until she dealt with the ones on her desk.

They needed her. They all needed her, and she couldn't help them all, which was why she'd become an attorney. But if she couldn't help Isaac, then how could she help the others?

She missed church to sit at the hospital, praying and hoping for a miracle.

"It looks worse than what it is," a nurse tried to assure her.

Between the hospital and her office, Emma hardly went home.

Vaguely, she remembered Rosco grabbing them dinners from someplace down the street last night.

She woke curled up to something—or more like *someone*—warm. She pushed up, spotted Rosco's darkened chin, and sighed.

Those deep blue eyes greeted her under hooded lashes. "Morning."

Slipping from his arms, she let his jacket fall to her legs. "You stayed." Even after everyone left, he insisted he stay with her. Holly and Haden had come by earlier in the evening and her father arrived right before visiting hours ended.

She glanced at her phone and jolted upright. "You're late. It's nearly six thirty!"

"Ken's back, and he's covering since I took a few days off."

"You did?"

Rosco eased her down on a couch in the nearby waiting room. Reaching up, he pushed away a strand of Emma's static-filled hair.

She must look a mess. Her hand went to her mouth. *Please, oh please, don't have let him see me drool in my sleep.*

"Come here." He drew her in, wrapped his arms around her. "I'll go get us some coffee, but first this."

His head dipped. Emma's breath caught. For the first time since they'd met, his lips found hers. She melted into the kiss. Gentle, tender, it almost made her want to cry. He cupped the back of her neck, taking his time to explore and invite.

Caught in the moment, Emma relaxed, taking his invitation to kiss him back. Feeling bold, she wound her arms around his neck, caressing his mouth with hers.

"Coffee." His mouth left hers and sounded raspy.

Opening her eyes at such an odd remark to say when kissing, Emma leaned back and gazed at him. Her pulse fluttered wildly. "Coffee?"

"I think it's time to get coffee."

Her arms slid from his neck and fell to her sides as he released her.

"O-kay," she mumbled.

Rosco lifted her chin to look at him. She tilted her head just a little, hoping he would take advantage and kiss her again.

Those deep blue eyes darkened, a slow smile forming. "Babe, if you keep looking at me like that, I'll want to do more than kiss you, and we can't have that. Not yet."

His admission caused funny things to happen inside her. She watched him rise and brush her cheek with his thumb. "I'll be back."

Wordlessly, she let him go. Her heart tried to take control of the funny things going on inside her. Since when could a guy's kiss cause her to lose all her senses?

She was due in the office soon. Lori suggested she keep clothes at the office rather than run home, and her coworker was a saint to suggest it. What would Danvers think if he heard of her meeting with clients in her blue jeans?

She had hours yet to worry about it. She found the restroom, walked by the nurses' station.

The antibiotics were slow to do their work. Isaac's immune system wasn't strong enough to handle the infection on his own. For the first time in her life, she wanted to beg and plead with God, to save this baby. It struck her as selfish. Why would God choose to help Isaac over any of the other babies?

"His plans are bigger than ours." She could hear her father's voice even as she tried to decide to call him.

He'd be awake, and she missed him from the short visit last evening. He'd met Rosco, offering his hand and his support to the both of them. Her father never judged her, and when he spoke with Rosco it warmed her. The three most important males in her life were all together. Her father whispered, "Bring him by once in a while, will you?" as he hugged her and took his leave.

She'd never heard her father say that about anyone.

Two weeks was hardly enough time to dream about marrying a guy, let alone to come to a feasible conclusion of falling in love with him.

But if that kiss had been any indication, her heart had made up its mind. And maybe that's what scared her—getting too attached, too soon. Would Rosco leave her once Isaac came home? What if something happened to Isaac and she lost them both?

She hadn't heard from Deb since the first day at the hospital. Not unlike her mother to disappear from time to time, but Emma had a bad feeling.

With Audra gone, her nerves had been on edge. How could she trust a stranger's word that her sister lived?

By now, her sister could have contacted her. *We all deserve a second chance, don't we?* For Audra, for Isaac. She stumbled in her mind to think of Deb. Forgiveness didn't mean forgetting. It didn't mean letting them back in your life to hurt you over and over again. But she had nothing to forgive Audra for. It wasn't her fault Deb was their mother. Whatever trouble had brought them to this place, it had brought Isaac into their lives. That couldn't be a bad thing, could it?

She stood and looked out the window of the waiting room. The aroma of strong coffee was the first to greet her. Then the warmth of the arm curling around her with a cup in hand.

She leaned back into Rosco, watching the town come awake, and wishing Audra could be here to see her baby, just this once for both their sakes.

———

Emma no sooner got into the office before Jacob Marrow
came knocking. "Hey, you got any other files on Everson?
Danvers said to see you."

"Ask Lori, but I'm sure everything we had she handed
over," Emma said, going back to finish writing this petition
before four o'clock. She needed Lori to proofread it before
heading out for the day.

"I heard you were cutting clients. You need me to pick up
any more?"

Emma slid her hands away from her keyboard. "I'm not
cutting clients. Everson doesn't like to be told he can't have his
way. I wish you the best with him."

Marrow tapped his fingers against her doorjamb. "I see."
He cleared his throat. "Well, Danvers suggested you might
need your client list lightened."

"Nope." Emma gave him her best high-wattage smile.
"I'm good. Thanks."

"You know where I am," he said, turning and heading
back out of her doorway.

Lori ducked her head inside. "You good?"

"Yep." Emma placed her hands back on her keyboard,
trying to remember where she left off on the petition.

"You used your extra outfit," she pointed out.

"I stayed late at the hospital."

Lori didn't budge.

"Okay, maybe the entire night. They're trying a different
antibiotic. He's not responding well to this one."

Lori stepped further into the office. "I'm sorry," she said
quietly. "Any news on your sister?"

Any mention of her sister had Emma picking up her
phone by her keyboard. Looking at the screen, she smiled at
the picture of Isaac, her, and Rosco.

Hours later, the memory of his kiss still lingered.

"Do you think there is more to it?"

Emma glanced up at Lori, her coworker's glasses shoved

up in her hair. Her face genuine with concern, Lori said, "What if she can't come back? Like a crime witness or something?"

"I've thought of that. Audra's always been a magnet for getting in trouble like our mother. It's more like she's hiding to keep from anyone prosecuting her."

"Well, we all know you can't run from your troubles."

Lori would know. She'd left her trucker ex-husband as soon as she got her degree and had a steady enough job to come work at the law firm. After running for years to escape him, finally, she stood her ground and found a new life here.

If only Audra would want the same.

It was all Emma could think of, that and Rosco. He got involved, and she feared she was relying on him too much. This morning, it felt like they had always woken up with her in his arms. And that kiss.

She rubbed her eyes. She couldn't afford to let him keep kissing her that way. She had to focus.

When her phone rang, Emma's heart skipped a beat. The number belonged to the detective in Audra's case.

Forgetting this was her personal phone and not her work phone, she answered, "Hello, Emma Harris."

"Miss Harris, it's Detective Griffith. I'm sorry to have to call you with bad news."

Instantly, her world started to shatter. *Please, God. Not Audra. Not Audra...*

"Miss Harris?"

She realized she hadn't spoken, hadn't twitched in the slightest.

"Yes?" She managed to find her voice, dread coiling inside her like a poison snake.

"Are you related to a Debra Phillips?"

A bit of the dread started to ease. "She's my birth mother."

"She was found badly beaten inside the back of her car

this morning. I thought you would like to know she has been taken to Conemaugh Hospital."

Emma's hand loosened, almost dropped the phone. She let it slide down onto her desk. Hit the speakerphone. Deb? Beaten?

She took a deep breath. Not Audra, but still, the news made her feel ill.

"I need to ask you when the last time you saw your mother was," Detective Griffith's voice came out of the speakerphone.

"Um... a few days ago. At the hospital." The same hospital her mother was at now. Emma squeezed her eyes shut. What had Deb gotten into? Was it money? Had she borrowed from the wrong people? What if she'd gotten involved with another dealer? She said she was going clean.

Emma tried to remember to breathe in through her nose and out her mouth. She shouldn't care this much, but it made her stomach twist.

"Did your mother mention anything about anyone who would want to cause her harm?"

Emma tried to recollect her last discussion with Deb.

"She just said she had places to go and people to see, which isn't unlike her."

"Have you ever known her to be associated with any bikers?"

"I–I don't know. Listen, Detective Griffith, Deb and I aren't close. As I told you, she's my birth mother. The fact she showed up at the hospital about the baby is a red flag to me. Deb only does things when it benefits her, that I can tell you."

And there she went, letting her emotions get in the way of facts again.

"I see." Obviously Detective Griffith didn't see, or he wouldn't have called Emma. But Deb might have listed her as next of kin.

"Do you think this has anything to do with my half-sister's disappearance?"

A long pause drew static over the phone.

Marrows walked down the hall, paused in front of the glass by her door. He turned his head, Lori behind him, and Emma held her breath waiting for a response.

"I can't say."

Except he had, in more ways than one.

Just breathe, Emma.

"My sister isn't coming home, is she?" It came out in a desperate hoarse whisper. The kind that slithered down one's throat and caught in their chest. The type that welled tears behind her eyes and had her glaring out toward the glass, where a confused man glanced her way, and Lori waited.

"In cases like this—"

She cut him off. "Don't. I work with child abandonment cases every day. This is more. This is my half-sister, and now Deb is involved. What aren't you telling me? I *know* she's alive."

"I understand how you must feel."

"No. You don't." She talked down to the phone.

"Your sister is a key witness in an ongoing investigation. We are doing everything we can to find her and ensure her safety. If you should hear from her, it's important to get in contact with me."

Emma covered her face with her hands, leaning her elbows on her desk. She peeked through her fingers at the phone. "Am I in danger?"

Audra could have dragged them all into this. First Isaac, then Deb.

"We don't believe so, but to be on the safe side, call me if anyone or anything out of the ordinary approaches you or happens."

"Sure."

And like that, the conversation was over, leaving Emma reeling in her office chair.

17

It was late by the time Emma made her way back to the hospital. With only an hour left of official visiting hours, she needed to see Isaac. The detective's call had unsettled her.

Rosco had sent her several text messages, and she'd ignored them all. Too many people she cared about had gotten hurt lately. *Oh Audra, what have you gotten us into?*

For almost a half hour after Detective Griffith's call, Emma had closed her door and sank to her knees. Burying her face in her hands, she prayed behind the door. Not because she cared if anyone saw her, but because she needed to be alone, with God, with the fear of losing Audra, losing Isaac, and now Deb crippling her.

Prayers said, she picked herself up off her knees and got back to work.

Going straight to the hospital from work, Emma inquired at the nurses' station to find Deb.

Rosco called and the vibration of the phone in her hand tugged at her heartstrings.

While riding in the elevator, another text dinged from her phone. Three messages from Rosco asking her when she got off work. Was she still working? Had she eaten yet?

The elevator came to a jolted halt. The doors slid open and she stepped out, making sure she was out of the way of anyone wanting to get inside, and texted him back.

Go to bed. I'm at the hospital and going home shortly.

She would, right after she saw Deb.

How is our little guy?

Emma stared at the phone. "He's not ours. He's not even mine," she muttered, texting him back.

Same.

She tucked her phone in her pocket before she got tempted to text him more. People were leaving a room across the hall. 840. She counted the numbers and found the dark room where her mother rested inside.

She didn't want to disturb her. A thought that she should have brought flowers flashed in her mind. Would Deb care that she came?

A nurse stepped out of the darkness. "Visiting time is almost over."

"I just need to check on her and make sure my mother is okay."

The nurse gave her a faint smile. From the look of her tired eyes, the dark-skinned woman must have been on her feet all day. Emma could feel her exhaustion creeping into her bones, cold and heavy. She dragged her feet stepping inside the room. Deb lay in the closest bed. A curtain pulled between the occupants.

Light overhead glowed softly to illuminate the older woman's battered face. Beneath the thin sheet and blanket, her mother's arm laid across her chest, wrapped in a cast. A monitor was hooked to her heart, and oxygen filtered into her nose.

"She's been sedated." A nurse appeared with a tray with a pitcher of water in her hand. She moved past Emma to the patient on the other side of the curtain. She heard the rustle, the murmur of another female voice.

Afraid if she sat, even for a minute, she would spend another night sleeping on hospital furniture, Emma stood at the foot of her mother's bed.

Her phone vibrated again, sending shock waves through her chest, tightening her throat and closing in her lungs. She hugged herself, rocking back and forth for a few minutes.

Her mother mentioned knowing Audra's boyfriend, knowing she was pregnant. Had Deb gone running to the bikers? Had the father of Audra's child done this to her mother? What would he have done then to Audra?

Would they come for her, or Isaac, or even Rosco next?

A shiver raced down her spine.

Maybe she should have brought flowers and left them by Deb's bed. It was too late to visit the gift shop.

Instead, she returned to the maternity ward and NICU. Emma headed to the nurses' station, wanting to let them know she'd call in the morning. She had court at nine a.m., and she promised her clients she'd be there to help them gain custody of their grandchild.

At the nurses' station, a man in a leather patched vest with steel-toed boots stood. Something seemed off about him. Maybe it was the way he looked at her, or the way his eyes traveled over her that made her wish she'd worn a thicker jacket.

"I'm sorry, visiting hours are over. As I told you, we can only release information to the family."

The man curled his big hand into a fist. Tattoos covered his knuckles, and he leveled his gaze on the middle-aged nurse. "I don't need a name or any of that, woman. Just tell me if the kid is still here."

Emma found the courage to speak. "I believe that's still a breach of patient privacy." The nurse, a face she had become acquainted with over the weeks, sat back down. She turned away, wanting to avoid the man, as much as Emma felt her fingers twitch.

The way his upper lip curled sent a cold drip through her veins. "You got a kid in there?"

"I'm a child advocate lawyer." Perhaps a big man like him would get intimidated with such a big title. People held many opinions of lawyers. She didn't like to judge anyone on the first impression, especially after Rosco had proved her wrong. Still, the man cracked his neck and took another lingering gaze at her.

"Kind of late to visit a client."

"Lawyer hours are much like doctors'. Perhaps if you have questions about a patient, you should seek their guardian."

He crossed his arms, big beefy arms that made her double think if she needed to take a step back.

"A friend of mine's old lady dropped a kid and ran, you understand?"

She tried. She wanted to, and the nurse peeked a glance at her, then moved away as another nurse came to join her. They stayed huddled at the far end of the counter.

"I'm sorry to hear that."

"One of you is going to tell me what I want to know." He glared over at the nurses.

"Perhaps he should try getting in touch with her or a lawyer. Are you with the biker club?"

"Yeah," he said. "What's it to you?"

"I don't remember seeing you with the others. What did you say your name was again?"

Cold, again, she wrapped her arms around herself.

"I didn't say." He stepped closer, and Emma stepped back. "I need to know about the kid, and you can find out for me."

He nodded toward the NICU, and Emma swallowed.

They all knew Isaac's name and his gender in the Thunder Valley MC. He kept his back from her view. Trying not to show her unease, she forced a smile. She couldn't see his patch, but the gruffness of his voice sent flags up in her brain.

"It's the premature one from the paper," he said, his voice low, harsh.

"Oh." it came out in a whoosh.

She dared a glance at the nurses. One moved off as the other hovered near a phone. Would they call security?

"You're a lawyer. You heard of him?"

"Well, y-yes. B-but I-I don't know. It's been rough these past few days. He's so little. He wasn't supposed to be born yet."

He nodded, satisfied with her answer. He grabbed her by the arm, startling her. "I don't like seeing babies die," he said.

"Me n-neither." She glanced down at his fingers biting into her arm.

"You make sure that kid is taken far away from here, you got me?"

"Yes." Emma stared at him, her insides twisting.

He relaxed his hold on her. "Don't make me come back here." He rolled back his shoulders and stalked away.

Her legs going weak, Emma grabbed hold of the counter.

On his back, the patch of a large shark fin made her feel as if she were drowning. Leaning into the counter, she took several deep breaths. One of the nurses came to her aid, but she waved them off.

"Are you okay?"

"I will be," Emma said, thinking, *Not really. Not ever.* She pressed her hand to her chest, trying to hold herself together. She fought scary people in the courtroom all the time, but never like this. It sliced her deep to the marrow. *Isaac…*

Lord, please give me the strength to do what I must to protect the people I love, even if it hurts them.

She looked at her phone, gazed at the photo of Rosco with her and Isaac. A text from minutes ago, one she missed, flashed on the screen.

Walking out of the hospital into the chilly October night, Emma clutched her phone. The entire way to her car in the parking garage, her body trembled. She walked fast, feeling someone watching her, but no one was there as she glanced around.

Inside her car, she locked the door and let the tremors rack down her back. She leaned forward, gripping her steering wheel. Her phone within reach, she debated calling the detective as she drove. Softly, she laughed as she imagined the conversation. What would she say? How would she explain? She had no tangible proof that would hold up in court or justify reporting it.

Turning on her headlights, she pulled out of the parking space and left the hospital behind her. Twenty minutes later, she pulled into her father's driveway.

No explanations, no words needed, he opened the door and did what he always did best. Emma sat at the counter in the kitchen while he stirred and made homemade hot chocolate over the stove. He slid her a sandwich. Unable to protest when he gave her that look, she sank further into her stool and picked out the tomatoes.

"You're more like your mother sometimes than you know," her father said.

"Can I stay the night?"

Her father pulled down two mugs and was far quieter than usual.

"Dad?" she asked, taking a bite into her sandwich, feeling young and vulnerable.

"You know where your room is." He poured the steaming mugs of hot chocolate and sat one in front of her. "You don't have to ask to come home, Emma."

"Thanks." She pulled the mug toward her, the steam warming her hands through the ceramic. She blew on the curling heat rising from the liquid.

Across from her, James Harris leaned over the counter, rested an elbow so he could level with her. He held his cup of hot chocolate tucked in his bent arm. He reached over and took her rejected tomato. "Things are getting real, and it scares you."

He popped the slice of tomato in his mouth, and Emma wished she could stuff her mouth with another bite of sandwich. Her father made the best turkey club sandwiches, minus the tomato, but her stomach wouldn't hold any more.

"It's Deb." She figured she should tell him. Sooner or later, he would find out, and she was in the mood to confess. Not *confess*—she shook her head—*share*. For so many years, she shared everything with him. Almost everything. Her lips threaded a small smile. She hadn't told him about the boys she crushed on, but he knew the grief she experienced not having a mother around.

"What about Deb?" Her father's voice deepened.

"She's in the hospital." And Emma filled her father in about the call from the detective, checking on Isaac, and looking in on Deb while she was there. What she hadn't told him about was the odd meeting with the biker. She didn't want to worry him.

"I'll go in tomorrow to see her." Her father took a seat beside her. Suddenly, he seemed pale, washed out. .

She laid her hand on his arm. "You've been working long hours again?"

He covered her hand with his. "I was planning some time off. Thought I'd head down to Florida to visit your Aunt Monica."

"Why didn't you tell me?"

He patted her hand. "You've got so much going on. I figured you couldn't get away, and I'm not sure if going now is a wise idea. Maybe I'll wait until closer to the holidays. She asked about you. I told her you had a man in your life."

"Really, Dad?" She hoped he was talking about Isaac because right now, that baby boy was everything to her. More than she wanted to admit, Rosco meant something too. Most men ran when they saw single mothers or the thought of raising someone else's baby.

"You've got that look in your eye, Twinkles," James said.

"Stop." She wasn't a fan of that nickname.

"Deb's going to be okay. She's a tough old bird, but don't you be like her. I've seen that look, Emma. I saw it on your mother's face the day she handed me a six-week-old baby and ran."

"I'm not running." She gazed into the swirls of her hot chocolate.

"Then what are you doing?" her father asked.

Emma looked at him. "I'm doing what I do best. I'm looking out for the other people around me."

James's arm went around her shoulders. "That's my Emma. Just remember, Twinkles, you're not alone. God's got this. You just have to give it over to Him." James kissed the top of her head as he stood.

She gave her father's hand one last pat. After her father cleaned up her half-eaten plate of sandwich and took his hot cocoa back to his den, Emma retreated to her room.

You're not alone.

She changed into a pair of flannel pants and a long sleeve T-shirt she kept there. Falling back on the teal comforter, Emma stared at her phone. She started to text Rosco, backspaced twice, and muttered, "Coward."

Rolling over on her side, she watched the screen light up, the picture of them, until the phone blinked out. Her mindset was on what she needed to do.

———

"Tiger." Sebastian gripped the door.

"Gonna invite me in, bro?" Tiger took hold of the door, the butt of a gun sticking out between the waistline of his pants and his shirt.

"I'm kinda busy." Sebastian raised to his full height so Tiger couldn't look inside.

"Is that right?" Tiger stepped closer. Body odor and spilled alcohol wafted from him. Sebastian held his ground. Behind him, something brushed across the worn carpet. Inside, Audra was trapped with no other exit.

He had made sure no one could have followed him.

Sebastian's jaw clenched.

"This is a real interesting setup you got going." Tiger grinned, the bastard. He leaned in, "No wonder Griffith called me."

None of the others heard him. Puffer and Chum lingered several feet back. In the parking lot, only one of them had ridden on a motorcycle. A dark SUV was parked directly in front of the motel door, with Hammer in the driver's seat.

"You're the contact?" Sebastian bit his tongue in an effort not to swear, keeping his voice low. Trying to keep his cool, he watched as the others tilted their chins up and leveled their gazes at him. Puffer's bald head gleamed under the lights shining down on the parking lot. Chum shifted weight to his other foot.

Razek hinted to him weeks ago there was another inside man. He wouldn't have suspected Tiger. What was Griffith doing on the case?

Sebastian glanced back at Audra. She'd grabbed the bag, stuffed a few things in, and backed toward the windows near the bathroom. Sebastian peered around Tiger. "What you need them for?"

His gut told him something wasn't right. Why would Tiger bring the other two along?

Tiger grinned. "They're your redemption, or at least your buddy, Chum. What do you think Pike's going to say when he finds out you've been hiding out with Dory? He's going to bust you up good, man." Tiger moved forward, but Sebastian wouldn't budge.

Behind him, he heard Audra's half cry muffled. He kept his eyes locked on Tiger.

"He'll kill her," Sebastian hissed.

Tiger reached for his gun. "She's bad for business, and business been good. You get me?"

Something in the edge of Tiger's voice had Sebastian keeping his eye on the gun in the other man's possession. "Yeah, man, I get you."

Four against one, counting the driver.

"Good. She tell you anything?"

So that was it. Pike needed Audra quieted. About which part of his business? Or all of it?

"I thought Griffith would have told you."

"He told me enough to know where to find her. Now, this can go down one of two ways, either one, she has to come with me."

"And them?" Sebastian asked, contemplating slamming the door shut, but Tiger's foot had edged to the door. Puffer came closer, reaching behind him.

"Leave those two behind, and we'll take her in together," Sebastian said.

"I don't think you understand who is in charge here, *pawn.*" Tiger yanked the gun out and jabbed it into Sebastian's chest.

Automatically, Sebastian froze. His breath caught in his lungs. Behind him, Audra whimpered.

"Move out of the way." Tiger pressed the gun harder into his chest.

"I can't do that. I can't let you take her back to Pike. It's a death sentence, and you know it."

Tiger twisted the end of the gun against his flesh, and Sebastian gritted his teeth. "There is only one way this can end."

Tiger shoved on him, and Sebastian stumbled back. Pike's lackeys closed in on him.

"No! I won't go back!" Audra yelled.

Sebastian slipped to the side, swung, and caught Tiger against the jaw. His hand hit the door, and Audra screamed as the gun went off, heat slicing through Sebastian's leg. He twisted, taking Tiger down with him. A hand on his neck squeezed off his air.

He gripped Tiger's wrist, kicking up his leg, trying to unbalance the larger man.

"Get the girl!" Tiger yelled at the other two.

Sebastian choked, the words barely audible. A wave of dizziness swept through him.

Audra backed away. Like a caged animal, she ran toward the windows.

Sebastian blinked, trying to hold consciousness. He stuck his leg out, tripped up Puffer as he crossed to get to Audra.

Chum hovered behind Tiger, staring down at Sebastian, his eyes widened.

"What are you looking at?" Tiger asked.

Chum slammed into Tiger, sending the two rolling against the bed. Sebastian went to his side, crawled up on his knees.

Puffer strode toward Audra. Sebastian lurched forward, wrapped his arms around the large biker's neck.

"Go!"

Audra headed out the door at the sound of knuckles hitting flesh, and a man's grunt came from the side of the bed. Tiger looked up, scrambled to reach for the gun. Chum dived at the same time. Puffer elbowed Sebastian in the ribs. Pain sizzled up his side, his grip loosened, and he took another blow in the stomach.

Sebastian stumbled back.

"Get her! Don't let her get away!" Tiger shouted.

Chum jumped on top of Tiger and the two went for a roll, the gun still in Tiger's hand. Puffer kicked Chum, sending the man sprawling off Tiger.

Puffer pulled his gun, pointing at Audra running out the

door. Sebastian moved for the weapon, blocking the shot. He forced Puffer back, knees buckling against the bed, and the gun went off. The shot went high, splintering into the doorjamb.

Seeing Audra flee, Tiger directed the gun back to Sebastian. "You're one dumb brother."

Pain exploded in his head.

18

Rosco sat and waited on Emma's porch steps. He'd sat down the pizza and the flowers beside him. He checked the hospital, and the nurses said she'd come earlier. No one could hold Isaac, so Rosco had given the infant a pep talk through the glass.

The new antibiotics seemed to make an improvement. The baby's progress was slow, but the staff had said if the baby continued to improve, he'd come home by Christmas.

Rosco checked his phone again. As he tried to call Emma one more time, it went straight to voicemail. "Emma, it's Rosco. I'm worried, and I want to make sure you're okay."

He hung up. Where could she be?

Darkness fell over an hour ago, and like an idiot, he'd sat on her porch waiting and hoping for her to come home.

Emma hadn't replied to any of his messages the last few days, either. Each time he called, it went to voicemail. He called her work and got one of the administrative assistants, who would only tell him Emma was in court, which meant she'd showed up for work. Otherwise, his next call would have been the police to report her missing.

Why wouldn't she return his messages or calls?

Of all the girls to give him the brush-off, Emma hadn't seemed the type. What had he done?

At least she'd spared him the 'let's be friends' talk.

Had she found someone else?

She was too worried about her sister, about Isaac. No, she wouldn't do that to him.

He left the pizza and the flowers and headed to her office. Her car wasn't in the parking garage. He drove to Deb's street, tried to remember which house. In the dark, with all the houses almost identical, it was practically impossible.

He tried to retrace his steps, parking across the street. Rosco walked over to the sidewalk. One house remained in the dark—no lights on inside. The door beside it opened. He took a chance and walked up. "Excuse me. Can you tell me if Deb Phillips lives here?"

The man grunted. "Don't know. Don't care."

Rosco thanked him and moved on. Across the street, a woman pulled out her trash, and Rosco went to help her. He lifted the heavy bag and set it out by the road.

"Thank you," she said. In the house, a dog barked and the television played.

"You don't perhaps know a Deb Phillips, do you?"

The woman closed her housecoat and took a step back from him. "What you want with ole Deb?"

"I'm a friend of her daughter's. I haven't seen her in a while, and I'm worried."

The woman nodded. "Ain't seen Deb for a few days. I don't know anything about her daughter. The last time I saw Deb, she was going on about being a grandma and getting paid to take care of the kid, so she didn't have to work anymore. Something about the daughter ran off." The woman took a step closer to him, looked at him real hard. "You the father?"

"No." But he wanted to be. He could picture Isaac in Emma's arms, them on a Friday night cozied together in the living room. In such a short time, they'd both wiggled deep down in his heart.

"Well"—the woman straightened herself up—"Deb still owes me for the crib. You tell her when you find her not to go blowing all the money from the baby daddy and pay up, you hear?"

"Yeah. I'll do that." Rosco watched as the woman went back inside.

His phone vibrated, and Emma's number flashed across his screen. Answering right away, he listened as she sobbed.

"Emma? Is that you? What's wrong? Where are you?"

She must have butt-dialed him or something. He could hear her muffled cries, and it tore him in two. "Emma?"

"Rosco?" Her voice was barely audible over the phone.

"I'm here." He came around as if she'd see him standing there in the dark by his truck.

"I'm sorry," she whispered. "I didn't mean to call."

"Just tell me what's wrong. Where are you?"

She sniffled. "My dad's. I'm staying with him. For now."

"What happened?"

"I'm sorry. I shouldn't have called."

"Wait! Emma, don't hang up. You know I'm here for you and Isaac. You can call me any time. I was at your house. I've been worried. Please, baby, talk to me. I want to see you. Where does your dad live?"

The line went quiet. He cupped his hand around the back of his neck.

"I d-don't know."

"You don't know where your dad lives?" he asked, finding a bit of amusement in her confession.

She sniffled again. "I can't do this. I'm sorry. I don't want to get you involved."

"Emma!" he growled, yanking open the door of his truck. "I've been all over town trying to find you. I went to your house, the hospital, your office, and even your mother's house. Give me the address. I'm coming to see you."

"Deb's not home."

"You know where she is?" He paused from starting up the truck.

"She's in the hospital, Rosco. Those bikers beat her up really bad. Audra must have called her. She knew where Audra was, and she tried to sell them information. She sold out her own daughter."

Yeah, that was bad.

"Emma…" He was lost for words. It killed him inside. The pain in her voice gripped him.

"Don't come to the hospital to see Isaac anymore. One of them was there. They know he's there. I-I don't think it would be wise for us to see each other anymore."

See him anymore? She admitted they were dating. "I think I have the right to decide for myself who I see and who I don't, and right now, I want to see you, Emma."

God, please don't make me beg.

"I-I like you, Rosco. Too much. I couldn't bear it if anything happened to you."

Like him?

God, he loved this woman.

"Emma, I—"

But she'd hung up.

He lowered the phone, stared at the screen as the light went to dark. He sat in the truck. Slammed a fist on the steering wheel, hit the horn. Jolted by the sound, he sat up straighter and drove away before he called any more attention to himself than necessary.

———

"So, you're giving up? I thought you liked this girl." Nicole stood by the microwave out in the hallway of the company offices.

"What would you have me do?"

"Show up at her work? She goes to the hospital. Wait for her there."

"Done both. She's got me on the 'do-not-allow-in' list. And her mother, Deb, wasn't much help."

"You visited her mother?" Nicole popped open the microwave door as it beeped.

"I took her flowers."

Nicole reached up and patted his cheek. "What a sweet son-in-law you are."

"We're not married." He crossed his arms.

"Yet." Nicole pulled out the cup of soup. The entire hallway smelled of clam chowder.

"I've only known her for two weeks." In such a short amount of time, he'd gotten attached.

"Did you go to her father's place?"

"I don't know where he lives."

"What's his name?" She stirred and blew on her soup. He knew that look. "Her last name is Harris." She shrugged, heading back to her office. "How many of them can there be?"

"A lot." He wasn't sure this was a good idea, but it was all he had.

"Know his first name?"

Rosco took a deep breath and let it out slowly. The more Nicole tried to help him, the more frustrated he felt.

"Why aren't you out in the shop with Lucas?" Brian ducked his head in Nicole's office.

"Geez, Brian, give the guy a break. We're doing stuff here." Nicole sank into her office chair. "You don't know any Harrises, do you?"

"What's that got to do with anything?" Brian came inside, his sleeves rolled up at the elbows and papers in his hands.

"Rosco needs to find Emma."

"Don't you know where she lives by now?"

So, Nicole took the liberty of filling their older brother in on Rosco's dilemma. Brian softened. "That's rough. Give her space. I'm sure she'll come around."

"Or move on." Nicole clanked her soup cup on the desk.

"It sounds like Emma is going through a lot right now. I'd give her a breather. If it's meant to be, she'll come back around. You can't force things to happen the way you want them to happen." Brian made a face at Nicole.

Those two rarely agreed on anything.

"Just be her friend." Brian shrugged, "And get back to those dumpsters. I need to place five by Friday."

"I'll look up Harris. If you remember the dad's name, let me know. We'll find her. Don't give up. Emma might be going through something but leaving her alone is a guy thing. Girls need to know they got someone, and especially if she feels responsible for a lot of stuff." Nicole flipped open her laptop. "She could just be scared."

"I know." Rosco headed out to work on the dumpster. Something had spooked Emma, and it made him feel a tremendous urge to find her.

———

Sebastian's head throbbed. Groaning, he held his head, afraid it would split in two. As his vision came back, slowly, he blinked. The throb at the side of his head went down to a ringing in his ear.

Cold leaves pressed against his cheeks, and pain radiated up his side. A faint light flickered between the tree limbs above. It took a few moments for him to get his bearings. Judging by the light, it was still morning, the sun still rising.

Tremors swept over his body from the chill. How long had he laid out in the elements? Bile rose in this throat, and he pushed it down.

He heard the muffled cries but couldn't place them. "Audra?"

Was that rough gargled sound his voice?

He struggled to sit up, brought up short as something moved in the leaves not far from him. Audra was tied to a tree at his feet. Her watery gaze met his, twisted his gut, and made him more nauseous.

Looking around, he spotted the back of a Shark-patched jacket and a bald head. Puffer. Sebastian gritted his teeth, forced his cold limbs to move. Slowly, ever so slowly, he bit back the shout pressing at his lips to raise. On his hands and knees, he crawled to her.

Her knees curled up, her hands behind her back, the thick rope wrapped around her chest several times and knotted behind the great oak.

She sucked in a breath.

"Shh." He tried to keep from rustling the leaves. "I'm going to get you out of this."

Her lips, a paler shade of blue than her hair, trembled. Despite the cold trying to lock up the muscles in his body, he managed to shed his coat. He tucked it around her.

"He's going to kill me. Please," she whispered. "The picture in my room of Emma and me. You have to give her the picture. Promise me."

"You can give it to her yourself."

Audra shook her head, shivering. Sebastian scooted closer; the sound of a twig snapping beneath his weight was inevitable.

"I'm going to untie you. I'll distract Puffer while you—"

Sounds of someone walking up behind them. "Well, isn't this cozy."

Pike's voice dripped like ice going down Sebastian's back.

Audra wet herself, her eyes dilated. "P-please…" It came out strained from her lips.

"Boss!" Puffer called.

Sebastian's legs cramped as Pike walked around, Tiger joining him.

"Didn't I tell you the two love birds would want to be together?" Tiger chuckled. He'd traded his handgun for a Winchester. It laid cradled in the crook of his arm.

Pike grabbed Sebastian by the throat, hauled him to his feet. Audra whimpered, pressing back further against the tree.

"You got some nerve coming into my pod, tailing my girl. Were you tailing her before you decided to join? Or after?"

Sebastian clung to the man's hands around his neck. He struggled to breathe, his lungs burning from the lack of oxygen.

"Nobody messes with what is mine." Pike's grin turned ugly. Black dots swam in Sebastian's vision.

"You kill him like this, we'll have to bury the body," Tiger said.

"Kill him," Puffer said. "I'll help dig the hole."

Sebastian jerked his body, no longer able to breathe, then all of a sudden, Pike released him. He crumbled at the biker president's feet, choking and coughing as he worked to inhale fresh air. His lungs expanded, causing pain to flare through his chest.

Pike strode over to Audra. "You're next, Dory, but first, you think you can get away from me? I'll show you what happens when you tease a Shark."

Pike grabbed the Winchester. Audra gasped, no longer crying. Sebastian figured she'd gone into shock.

Pike pointed the gun toward him. "You could have been a brother. I would have named you Spike. Shame you're a beast, and there is only one thing to do with a *beast*. Run, animal, Run."

Tiger grabbed Sebastian by the arm, helped yank him to his feet. "Griff's on his way."

Sebastian looked at him strangely, thinking he got hit harder in the head to be hearing things, then Tiger shoved him forward and said louder, "But he can't outrun a bullet."

Sebastian stumbled, took off as Pike rose the gun to aim. He veered left for the cover of a tree.

Oof—he heard the grunt, or was it his?

The rifle shot rang through the forest, splintering a tree several feet away. Sebastian looked back. Tiger and Pike rolled on the ground. Sebastian turned, as Puffer headed for the rifle.

Reaching behind his back, Sebastian swore: his gun was gone. He didn't wait to give Puffer a chance to get off a shot. He plowed into the big guy, sent him and the gun sprawling.

Audra whimpered as Pike flipped Tiger over, called him a few choice words, and slammed his fist into Tiger's face.

Sebastian tried to pin down Puffer, but the large man tossed him off, and Sebastian landed near the rifle. He reached for it when a foot came crashing down on his arm, the bone snapping and Sebastian screaming. He rolled away, using his feet to catch Puffer and bring him down.

On his knees, Puffer grabbed and twisted Sebastian's bad arm, the pain nearly sending him back to the world of darkness.

He heaved over, about to become sick, when he flung his head back, heard the crunch, and Puffer stumbled away from him. He grabbed the rifle, spun, and hit Puffer, knocking the man out. His large body fell to the ground.

Audra screamed. Pike and Tiger circled each other, Pike with a long blade in his hand. Adrenaline helping him to raise the heavy Winchester in his good arm, Sebastian aimed. "Put the knife down, Pike. It's over. You're under arrest."

Slowly, Tiger crouched, pulling a knife from his boot. He stepped back, holding up the blade.

"You're outnumbered," Pike sneered, twirling his blade.

"Am I?" Sebastian asked.

Pike's expression darkened. "You should have run when you had a chance. Now, I'm going to cut you up."

Sebastian cocked the gun. "Drop the knife, Pike."

Tiger moved to the tree, sawing through the ropes to release Audra.

"What are you doing? Helping him?" Pike's fist tightened around the knife handle.

In the distance, the sirens of cop cars came within hearing. Pike's face reddened. "You think you got me, but you don't. She won't say a word, not if she wants that brat to live."

Tiger cut Audra's hands free, and she stood, still leaning against the tree.

Not bothering to correct him, Sebastian focused on keeping the rifle in place. Sounds of people rushing down through the woods caused Pike to tense.

"You won't touch him!" Audra yelled, grabbing the knife from Tiger and running toward Pike. He grabbed her hand, twisting and shoving the knife in her chest. Sebastian's trigger finger jerked. Audra gasped. Tiger caught her as she fell back against him.

The rifle dropped from Sebastian's hands as police officers ran toward them. "Police, put down your weapons!"

Pike lay face-first on the ground.

"We're cops," Tiger shouted, holding onto Audra as Sebastian was forced to his knees, only able to hold up one arm.

"We're undercover. I'm detective Tyron Mills, and this is my partner. I'm the one who called it in to Griffith."

And just then, Detective Griffith walked out from behind them to confirm their story. "Get some EMTs here, pronto!"

Sebastian moved over and took Audra from Tiger's arms. Her head rested on his knees, and another officer looked at the knife embedded through her heart.

"It's going to be okay." His cold hands trembled, pushing her hair from her eyes. Those watery, innocent eyes, beseeching him and pulling at his soul.

"You shouldn't have attacked him."

"My baby is safe now. Isaac." She stared up at him, a faint smile ghosting her lips. Her color fading, she grew paler. He reached for his discarded jacket, pulled it over her.

"EMTs on the way."

Tiger glanced over at him, gave his head a slight shake.

Several cops surrounded Pike.

They dragged Puffer away as Sebastian strained to hear the ambulance. Where was it? It wouldn't make it in time.

He took her hand, colder than his. "Stay with me, Audra. Help is coming."

"The. Picture. Emma. Isaac. Safe."

19

The last thing Emma prepared before leaving work had been a petition to the court to allow a young girl's grandmother to have custody while the mother spent time in prison. She wrote it with numb tingling certainty. She would soon have to petition the court on Isaac's behalf with Audra gone.

Gone.

It felt surreal.

The phone call. The arrangements. Deb's usual demeanor was crushed with the loss of her daughter.

"Hey. I thought Danvers told you to leave and take off the rest of the week."

Lori came into her office. No new stacks of files. She gave two more clients to Jacob. Not her choice, but a necessity.

"I finished Mrs. Cole's petition. I just forwarded the file to you."

Lori's face pinched. She wanted to say something. Emma could practically see the words on the tip of her coworker's tongue but knew enough to hold them back. Nothing anyone could say would have her leaving this office without following through on the promises to her clients she'd made.

Besides, it made her feel in control of at least one situation in her life. She promised to help these people, and she wouldn't let them down. Those children deserved stability, security, and she would do her best to help them. She would protect them.

It clamped in her chest, squeezed the part of her she figured broke into a dozen pieces the day Audra died.

"What?" she asked softly, slowly bringing herself to close the laptop and sink into the desperation of leaving work, leaving the thing that kept her busy and not having to think about what came next.

"There's someone here to see you."

Her pulse kicked in, the first normal reaction she'd felt all day. She'd been going on autopilot since yesterday afternoon. It blurred in her mind, too fast for her brain to hold onto the words the detective spoke. Emma visited the hospital to see Isaac when her father accompanied her to share the news with Deb.

Guilt struck Deb.

Anger brought back those old feelings she once held against her mother. It was too late. Her mother would have to learn to live with the consequences of her actions, just as Emma would.

Audra would never meet her son.

Emma's throat clogged, and she shook her head. "I've already spoken with the detective. I just want to go home."

Not to her father's house. Not this time. She wanted to be alone.

"It's a guy with a motorcycle vest. I think he's been here before," Lori said, her eyes more than her voice radiating with sympathy.

Rosco. She'd told him days ago they couldn't see each other anymore. It felt like longer. But it was the only way she knew to keep him safe. She'd gone as far as to take him off the visitor list for Isaac and change her visit hours to avoid running into him.

No matter how much she'd come to care for him, it would have never worked out between them.

They were too different, and the thought of a motorcycle gang brought sickness to her stomach. A biker had killed her sister.

Even though she'd met the club Rosco was in and the kind people who prayed for her, for Audra, and Isaac, it twisted her up inside. How could two groups of bikers look the same but act so different?

The Thunder Valley club members wore the patch of a cross, and their mission was to help people grow close to Christ.

Right now, she didn't feel close to God. If anything, she felt further from him than ever. How could *he* have allowed this to happen?

Rosco hadn't deserved for her to push him away. They'd gotten close in such a short amount of time, and it scared her. Everything was happening too soon, too fast, and out of her control.

For a moment she put her hand on the corner of her desk, feeling as if her world was spinning.

It wouldn't work, she reminded herself again. Half-heartedly. She couldn't be the one left to pick up the pieces like her father had when Deb abandoned their relationship and left a baby for him to raise. She had to think of Isaac and what was best for him.

Thinking of Rosco complicated things worse. This was why she never dated anyone. This was why she should have never thought they could be friends. That kiss had changed things between them.

"Tell him I've already gone." A lie, one she hoped never to get caught in telling.

"I won't take long. I promise." Beast stepped into her office, and Lori stepped out of his way.

"He showed me his badge and said it was police business."

Behind him, Rosco stepped just within the doorway.

Her heart skipping several beats, she asked, "What are you doing here?"

"Giving a friend a hand," Rosco said.

He wore a navy hoodie with the Reynold's logo near his heart. His jeans were stonewashed, and his work boots scuffed. He stuck his hands in his pockets, his expression one of a man who'd been defeated.

Beast, the man who'd visited her office once before, stood with a cast on his arm and a sling holding it against his chest. His face was bruised, along with several days of growth that had sprouted on his chin. His eyes were sunken and his face thin and pale.

She knew he'd been there when Audra died.

"We would have waited and gone to your house, but your father said you'd be here," Rosco said.

"You saw my father?" Emma held onto the desk for support. Lori smiled and quietly stepped around the men, leaving Emma to her private business.

"He was with your mother when we went to go check on her," Rosco said.

Static filled the air in her office as if one word would shatter them all.

"I'll just wait down the hall while you two have a chat."

It killed Emma to see him walk away. It was her, after all, who'd been ignoring him, telling him to stay away. "No. Stay."

"Are you sure?" Rosco asked.

"Please." She expected him to give her space, especially after he stopped calling her a few days ago. She found the flowers and the stale pizza on her porch. She deserved to have him return the silence she gave him.

"Emma. My name is Sebastian, or you might have heard some call me 'Beast.' It's my road name with the motorcycle club. I was undercover trying to bring down the Sharks when we previously met."

She nodded, remembering, not sure where this was going or what to say.

"The police went back to your sister's residence. Her roommate had boxed everything up, and someone else was in her room."

It figured. Audra's roommate wouldn't even give Audra the time to return before tossing her out for someone new to move in.

Emma took a deep breath. "What can I help you with?"

Sebastian adjusted the strap of his sling and winced. He should have been resting, healing from the break and the wounds, but his face looked haunted.

"I'm looking for a photo. Audra said to give it to you and —" He paused, squeezing his eyes shut, his jaw twitching. Rosco laid a hand on his shoulder, gazing over at Emma, imploring her to have patience and something more. Something that made her walk around her desk and pick up the photo she'd found in Audra's room at the college apartments.

"We couldn't find it," Rosco told her. "The police searched through everything at the apartment. I remembered the day we went there, and the photo of the two of you. Do you still have it? "

"I do."

"What Sebastian is trying to tell you is that your sister wanted you to have it, but we think there's more to it."

She held the photo, showed it to the tormented man with the broken arm. "This photo? It's the only one I have of her recently. Why would she care if I had it?"

"May I see it?" Sebastian held out his good hand.

She gave it to him, watched as he inspected the frame. He moved closer to her desk, laid the photo facedown, and felt along the back. "Would you mind helping me with this? I think there is something in the back of it."

She used the tips of her fingernails to pry open the tabs in the back. Lifting the thick piece of board holding the photo in, she turned it around. A part had been carved out on the side, and a tiny disk lay nestled inside.

"It makes sense," Sebastian said, taking out the disk. "She knew if you had it and found it, you'd do the right thing. You're a lawyer. She probably figured you could put it in the right hands."

"What is it?"

"Evidence, I'm guessing the files burned on this disc came from Pike's computer. We'll finally be able to finish taking him down."

"I thought he was dead." Her nose tingled and burned as her sinuses clogged up for another good cry.

"He is." Sebastian's voice strained. "There's a bag in my pocket. Can you help me put it in there?"

"Of course." She helped him, pulling out a plastic bag and slipping the disc in. She slid it back in his pocket.

"This will help us take down anyone else he was working with, so thank you."

She didn't know what to say to that. A life to stop the corruption of the city. Since when had she become so poetic?

"Will you be going back undercover?" Curiosity made her ask.

"My biker days are over," he said.

"Mine, too," she said more to herself than him. A vice clamped around her chest and made it harder to breathe.

"Under other circumstances, I'd agree. They're a rough bunch. Some. Not all. There are ones who have paid the time for their crimes, and we shouldn't keep making them pay when they're trying to turn their lives around. And there are those who just love to ride and help others."

"You speak of Thunder Valley."

"They're a good bunch of people," Sebastian said. "They'd give you the shirt off their back if you needed it."

"I know." And, somehow, she did, really did know. She

looked at Rosco. She needed to explain and hope he understood. But mostly, she needed him.

"Emma." Sebastian squeezed his eyes again.

"Is your arm paining you?" She trembled, the numbness inside her quickly fading as she worried. He came here too soon after his injuries.

"I'm sorry," he said, his voice low, grieved. Quietly, she watched him go, Rosco right behind him.

The picture of her and Audra in her hand.

———

All the members of the Thunder Valley Motorcycle Club showed up for Audra's funeral, including Rosco. Instead of wearing his vest, he donned a suit. It stretched across his shoulders and tailored down his legs. He replaced his work boots with a pair of black dress shoes with laces, and he'd recently gotten a haircut.

Emma stood with her father. Deb remained in the hospital with a bruised spleen and broken hip. In the past few days, Emma's mother had aged considerably. Audra's death had sobered them all.

Rosco stayed in the back. Beside him, another man in a suit, and a woman she recognized as Rosco's sister, Nicole, stood along with him. Haden and Holly came with the Thunder Valley members, along with an older man in a wheelchair. Emma realized that man was Holly's father, still recovering from a motorcycle accident months ago.

They'd come even when they hardly knew her, hardly knew her sister. James Harris rested his arm around her shoulder, pulled her in tighter.

November blessed them with a warm day of rich, vibrant colors falling from the trees as the pastor of a local church spoke a kind message to give them comfort and assure them heaven had a place for her sister.

Around her, Audra had linked all these people together.

Emma ran out of tissues by the end of the graveyard service.

She preferred to stand back while her father took on all the hugs and handshakes. He acted as her shield. Too many hugs, too many squeezes and condolences. As the crowd thinned out, Emma chose to stay behind.

Holly and Nicole, and the other ladies she recognized from the night of her impromptu baby shower, gave her hugs and encouraging words. Half of them she wouldn't remember, but their kindness touched her. Lori and even Jacob Marrow left the office for the service.

"Whatever you need," Jacob said.

"I'm just a call away," Lori added.

Out of the corner of her eye, she spotted Rosco standing nearby, his lips thinned and his jaw tense. He rocked back on his feet as Jacob hugged her. It meant nothing, another embrace by those who knew her and not her sister.

None of Audra's school friends or even her roommate had come. Not one.

In the distance, Emma spotted a fellow with his hands in his pockets. Too far away, she couldn't make out his features, but he seemed familiar. Had he been the one who came that night to the hospital?

He seemed to sense her notice him and took off in another direction.

Walking up to the casket, Emma spotted the people coming to lower it. She had picked the petals from her flower and throwing dirt on Audra's casket just added pain to the open wound she carried. She took the photo of Isaac, one from the hospital and framed it for Audra. There hadn't been enough time for her to get it put inside the casket by the time she thought of it.

With limited funds, she opted to skip hosting a public

viewing. The local church volunteered to put together the meal.

She never understood how people could eat after burying their loved ones.

Yet, she waited and turned to find Rosco. Still in the same spot. He stood there, watching her watching him.

"How are you?" he asked, not saying with words what she could hear in his voice. The same thing whispered in her heart. *I missed you.*

"I've been better. You?"

"Same. A friend of mine lost her sister, and I feel like I've lost her," Rosco said.

"I'm sorry." She wanted to say more but didn't know how. Tentatively, she took a step toward him.

"Me too."

And she took another step. "If this friend wanted to apologize and be friends again, would you let her?"

"No."

And his answer took her back. Jaw unhinging, she guessed she deserved it. She'd pushed him away. She avoided relationships, people died, they took off, and she should thank herself for avoiding the pain. Only the pain caught up, tethered her to this place and this man. What would she do without him? It scared her more than admitting she couldn't live without him.

Too soon, she chided herself. *You don't know him.*

But she did.

She knew he loved pizza and couldn't stay awake longer than nine at night. She knew he worked early and went out of his way to be at the hospital every day, to see her, to see Isaac. He called on others to help her when he couldn't. He made time to spend time with her, and all she wanted to do was keep him safe.

Her pulse pounded with the quickening of her heart.

People who don't want you in their lives don't go out of their way to put themselves in it Her father's words when she told him about breaking things off with Rosco. As if they'd been a couple. And more than friends.

"I'm glad you're doing well." He just said he wasn't, but she wanted to slip away where she could grieve more than her sister. "Thank you for coming today. It means a lot." And that was saying something.

"I don't want to be your friend, Emma. I've been friends plenty of times with girls, but you're different. I'm no choir boy, ask my family, and I've made plenty of mistakes. I've tried to make up for them, and when I do, I get pushed aside as nothing more than a friend or the in-between guy until another comes along and takes the girl."

That stopped her in her tracks.

"I've been trying to fit in with the wrong people for a long time, and you, and me, and even little Isaac. We fit. Please tell me, you feel it?"

She wore a black dress with black heels, sinking in the damp earth there in the cemetery. "I do."

Lord, please don't let this be where he walks away from me.

Rosco moved closer. "I understand why you pushed me away."

"You do?" She was feeling like a doe in front of headlights.

"I know about Deb and seeing about—" He swallowed hard, his eyes shifting over to the casket, then back at her. "I have feelings for you, Emma, and you wouldn't have pushed me away to try and protect me if you didn't care for me."

"I was scared." There, she said it and the rest came spilling out. "First, with Audra missing, and I knew she was in trouble. I knew she was hiding from something bad, and the police even told me as much, but I couldn't tell you. Then Isaac had a bad time, and Deb showed up in the hospital. And that man, he came to the hospital about Isaac. He was one of them. He—" She turned, looked around the cemetery.

Rosco took her in his arms, turned her back around. "I'm not going anywhere."

She crumbled in his embrace, and he held her like their lives depended on it.

"But now you don't want to be friends." She figured by now her reserve of tears had dried up, but a few more squeezed by.

"It's all or nothing, babe," he said, and she pulled back to look at him.

"I want everything. With. You. I want your friendship. Your love. I want marriage and family. Starting with Isaac. I want the good and the bad, and I promise you, I'm not going anywhere. I love you."

Oh, he'd said those words, and it nearly brought her to her knees.

His arms tightened around her, his head tilting, coming in for the kiss. She closed her eyes, waited for the gentle brush of his lips, but gentle couldn't brand her with a promise like he did.

He poured everything into their kiss that he wanted back from her. He gave her sunshine and roses. He opened her to the taste of honey and the possibility of a future while chasing away the dark places. She wrapped her arms around his neck, sliding her hands up into the short crop of his hair.

Their kiss deepened, behind them the shuffle of the grave keepers, the rustle of leaves in a gentle breeze that grazed both their cheeks. He was solid and strong and not going anywhere. Heat kindled and took hold as Rosco released her. His gaze smoldering with promise and conviction gave off a spark as he dove back in, his kiss more urgent than the last.

She matched it and raised it with a dose of courage to chase out the fear. His hands slid down over her back, pressing her closer, a mix of joy and grief sliding into home.

A place made of love and sorrow. New beginnings and being brave for what lie ahead.

Rosco pulled back as the sound of dirt hitting the coffin had her holding onto him. He slipped his fingers between hers, bringing her hand up to his lips for a chaste kiss. "What do you say we go check on Isaac?"

"I'd say I'd like that very much."

20

Smoke curled and rose in thin streams from the garage. The fire trucks all left, but for one, watching and dousing and making sure the fire stayed out. What was left of Brooks Motorcycle Garage smoldered, leaving the scent of ash and motor oil in its wake.

Sebastian slid out of the truck, grateful for Rosco providing him a ride. With his arm immobile for a few weeks more, he left the Rebel parked in the police impound yard until Haden could retrieve it.

Sebastian cupped the back of his neck with his good hand. The fire marshal spoke with two officers, who glanced over at the newcomers. He recognized him, giving a wave and staying back. Once they finished, Haden approached them.

"What happened? Anyone hurt?" Sebastian asked.

"They broke in during the night, doused the whole place with gasoline."

"Arson?" What other reason would the fire marshal linger with Officers Simmons and Holmes?

"Looks that way," Haden said. "It was a message, I'm sure of it."

"You think this is connected with the Sharks? Pike is dead. The others are in prison," Sebastian said.

"Not all." Rosco stuffed his hands in his pockets, rolled his shoulders forward.

"If they wanted revenge on me, then why come after the shop?" Sebastian asked.

The fire marshal and the two cops broke away from their chat near the smoldering building. They walked toward them, and Rosco went to speak to the marshal. He handed Rosco a paper, and the two cops waved as they went. "We're headed back to the station to file this, but we'll be in touch."

"Is anyone patrolling the area?" Sebastian asked, more than the discomfort of his broken arm bothering him.

"We got this, Daniels. See you back at the station soon," Officer Holmes said.

Rosco handed the paper to Haden. "Good thing you got insurance."

"I'm sorry," Sebastian said, walking around, afraid if he stood still his knees would buckle.

"It's not your fault," Haden said. "We'll rebuild. It's a blessing in disguise. The remodel will give us a chance to make the place more handicap accessible for Charlie to get around."

"I'm glad you're taking this in stride, but what about the bikes?"

Rosco and Haden exchanged a look between them. Rosco stepped back and went for a walk.

"My Scout?"

"It's like they were targeting Charlie's bike collection. I'm sorry, Beast. Once the insurance company gets here, I'll be able to assess the damage. We might be able to save the frame and rebuild it. Custom."

"Rosco knew before he came to pick me up?" Sebastian scratched the extra growth on his chin. Shaving one-handed proved more difficult than allowing it to prickle along his jaw.

"Yeah." Haden grimaced.

"I take it this is a cleanup party instead of a bunch of bros hanging out."

"It turns out to be both." Haden pulled on the zipper of his jacket. Large chunks of white snowflakes floated in the air. Between the smell of the burnt oil and the heaviness of the snow accumulation about to fall, Sebastian felt the pressure building between them.

"Well, tell me what I can do," Sebastian said.

"Keep the Rebel," Haden said.

Sebastian rolled his shoulders back, winced as pain laced down his side. "No, man, I can't do that." Not after everything that happened. "It's parked at the yard near the station. You can go pick it up any time."

His arm angled across his body. The last thing he could do was keep the only remaining motorcycle Charlie owned that hadn't been damaged.

"Charlie's word. Keep the Rebel. This time it's not a loaner. It's yours."

Emotion worked its way up through his chest. Sebastian bit the inside of his cheek, trying to control it.

He took a deep breath, feeling the snow land on his cheek, wetness sliding down.

"Fine, but I'm trading it back once my Scout is on the road again."

Haden grinned, held out his hand, and Sebastian took it with his good one. "You're on."

"You know I won't be able to stick around. I wasn't even out of the hospital yet, and Razek is talking of sending me away. If the Sharks did this, then I'm putting you all in danger by being here."

"Pike messed with our business before you got involved," Haden said.

Rosco started heading back their way. Cold setting in through his jacket, Sebastian tried to ignore the brisk November chill. "Yeah, but Pike is dead. Now it's personal.

Anyone else know my ride was here?"

"No. I kept your confidence like I said I would. Not even Holly or Rosco knew. I figured since Holly got away, this was another act against Charlie."

"It's been months. Pike would have sent someone months ago after it happened. No, this has to do with Pike." And Audra, but he wasn't ready to say her name.

"Larry said one of the pledges is petitioning to take Pike's place, but he figures, for the most part, they won' t have a choice but to disband. All their officers are in jail, and with the investigation, it wouldn't be wise of them to start up again."

Sebastian had a few ideas on who, but none of them strong enough to stand up to that kind of leadership. He hoped they would stay disbanded, but something deep inside him said he wouldn't be around to see to it.

"Where will you go?" Haden asked as they moved away from the smoldering building.

———

"You wanted to see me?" Sebastian had a feeling he knew why Chief Razek requested him. He heard about Tyron Mills, the man who worked undercover as 'Tiger' and helped take down Pike of the Sharks biker gang several weeks ago.

He'd spent the past few weeks in a daze, stumbling ahead, as he watched one friend stand alongside the woman he loved and buried her sister. In a few weeks, Rosco planned to pop the question and propose. They'd get married and adopt Audra's infant son, Isaac.

Life went on, but Sebastian couldn't see that far ahead.

A woman died because he failed to protect her.

"You heard what happened to Mills." Razek always did like to get straight to the point.

"Yeah," Sebastian said.

Razek tilted his head, assessed Sebastian for a cool moment. "He's dead."

It took a moment for Sebastian to comprehend the news.

"You're not going to say anything?"

Sebastian lifted a shoulder. "What should I say? I didn't know him that well. I didn't even know he was one of ours until the day of——" God, he still couldn't say it. He couldn't go back to that moment in his head when he failed, yet again.

"I understand this got personal for you, with your friends involved. I want you to take some time off, heal and get your head back, and due to the circumstances, I think it best you disappear for a while."

"I figured you wanted me to leave."

"I've made arrangements with a buddy of mine for you to stay at his place."

Sebastian glanced behind him. He'd remembered to shut the door. He didn't spot anyone near Razek's office as he came in, but Razek lowered his voice as he spoke.

"This friend," Sebastian asked, "wouldn't happen to want to give me a new identity, would he?"

"I'll leave that up to you, but you're in danger." Razek motioned for him to sit.

"No thanks." Running and hiding wouldn't help him forget what happened.

"Don't be stupid, Daniels. There was a bounty on Mills' head. There's a bounty on yours," Chief Razek said.

"Pike is dead, Puffer and several of the others are in jail. Who is going to come after me?" Sebastian countered. How many nights had he prayed they would? Prayed they'd come after him so he could take them all out, put them away, make sure he got every last one. But in the end, it wouldn't change the fact he wasn't able to save Audra.

No amount of nightly prayers or pleas with God had saved her.

Maybe he shouldn't have relied on God so much, or just

maybe God hadn't been listening. Sadly, no invisible force could bring her back.

That was the first thing he needed to get straight in his head. Maybe time off was exactly what he needed —permanently.

Razek leaned forward, put his elbows on the desk, watching him a long moment. "The same one who took out Tiger three days ago."

Sebastian shoved his hand in his pocket to stop from slamming a fist on the desk, or the wall, or anywhere else. He failed. Not just Charlie, or Audra, or even Haden. Now the force was down not one, but two law enforcers.

"You should have told me about Tiger," he said.

"He was in too deep to risk it. I also know you were talking to one of your friends."

"I never told him anything. You told me to go undercover. You knew I was part of the Thunder Valley Riders. I switched motorcycles. Mine was unique."

"Unique enough, they went after it. They knew before you took your pledge," Razek said.

"Tiger."

Razek nodded.

"And you sent me in anyway?"

"We needed a second person. It made sense."

"And you're sure it was a Shark who took Tiger down? He could have made other enemies."

"They left a calling card," Razek said. "Word is out. We figured they'd want revenge, but I wasn't expecting it this soon. Mills' wife and daughter weren't home, but they passed the motorcycles on the way back to the house. We've arranged a security detail to keep an eye on things for a while, make sure no one bothers them. Lacey is a senior in high school this year, Edie wants to let her finish school, and then they plan to move. I think it's best we move you, too."

Sebastian sucked in his breath. He'd volunteered and got

himself in this mess when the Sharks tampered with Charlie's ride and Thunder Valley's business. Sebastian had joined the club several years ago as part of his community service requirement. His fellow brothers and sisters in Christ became like a family to him while living in Johnstown.

"I've got a safe house set up and a new identification ready. It's all here in this envelope, sealed."

Sebastian let out a breath. "I appreciate what you're doing, but it's not necessary."

Razek stopped pushing the envelope in his direction. "Use your head, Daniels."

"I'm not running. You said yourself. Pike is dead. Puffer and a few of the others are in jail. Just the pledges and the old-timers are left. Technically, I could waltz in there and announce my leadership. I heard one of the guppies was trying to keep it together."

Leaning back in his chair, Razek gave him a doubtful look. "Before or after they blow your head off?"

"If someone came for Tiger, it was one of the guppies. Probably the one trying to take over while the others are out of the way."

"Maybe." Razek rocked back on his chair. "Someone ordered it from the inside, but we closed down their operation and seized the building."

Sebastian shook his head, thinking. "For all, we know Tiger could have made other enemies."

"Until we know for sure, I need you to lie low for a while. You're not from around here. Did you have someplace in mind? Otherwise, take the envelope. I've already submitted your vacation request."

Sebastian reached for the envelope. How could he take a vacation when a woman was buried six feet under and never got to hold her baby? And then what would happen after that? Come back? Transfer to another force?

"I'll take you up on the vacation. There's a place I've got

in mind." Sebastian swallowed hard. "But you should know, I'm not planning on returning. I'm done."

Razek stopped rocking. "I figured you might say something like that. So, I made some calls, in case. You've got six months. Then I can arrange a transfer for you. After that, I won't be able to help you."

Sebastian reached in his pocket for his badge and laid it on the desk. "I appreciate it, but I won't need it."

"Where are you going?" Razek asked.

"I think it is best if I don't say, but it won't be here." Too many memories haunted him.

"If anything happens—"

Sebastian waved him off. "I'll let you know."

Razek stood, offered Sebastian his hand. "I expect to hear from you at least within the next couple of weeks. Let me know you're alive."

The older man's hand tightened on the shake. Sebastian cleared out his desk while a few of his coworkers paused to watch him. They all appeared to want to say something, but he went about grabbing what was his, which amounted to nothing much. He wasn't one for keeping personal things on his desk.

As he left, one of the female officers stepped in his way. "You take some time off? My family has a cabin in New York. If you want, I could reserve it for a week or two."

"Thanks, but I'm good," he said, not wanting to hurt her feelings. He didn't date coworkers, and she'd been hinting before he went undercover.

She shrugged. "Enjoy your vacation."

Sebastian put on a smile for them and walked out before he changed his mind.

The last thing he wanted to do was end up somewhere with another woman depending on him for anything.

WHAT'S NEXT?

Three years ago, Caitlyn Cotes escaped from her abusive old man. Now he's back blackmailing her to help frame her best friend's brother if she wants to keep her son safe. Sebastian Daniels has a bounty on his head. He's a cop, and everyone knows what happens to cops in prison. Because one way or another, the members of the Sharks MC will have their justice.

Going back to his roots in Gettysburg, Sebastian refuses to hide. The ghosts of his past wait for him, and he can't be responsible for keeping anyone else safe.

The longer they spend together, the more Caitlyn is drawn to Sebastian, and if she's not careful, she'll lose the two people she cares the most about. Can she trust Sebastian to keep her son safe, or will the truth send them both spiraling down a dead end street?

SNEAK PEEK OF SEBASTIAN

Sebastian parked his motorcycle beside the shed in the rear lot of the vintage white church. He was early, and nervous, and wondered if he should ride out and circle back as to not seem too anxious for the job. He checked his phone, twenty minutes before he was told to show.

He took off his helmet, slid down and sat beside the Honda Rebel, careful to avoid the hot pipes. One leg bent, the other out straight, he scanned the area, taking note of the entrance and exit of the parking lot and the traffic on the road.

Soon the roar of a bike caught his attention. A silver Yamaha, slim and sleek like its rider pulled up, with a rider looking equally as petite. Parking next to the shed, she swung a long leg over the seat and stood.

Sebastian rose as the woman pulled off her helmet. The woman shaking loose her long, dark brown tresses. She kept her back to him, taking care of her gear. Reaching into a saddle bag, she pulled out a clipboard and some other papers.

The view from the backside wasn't all that bad, and when she turned, Sebastian met her sunglass covered gaze. "Sign in isn't for another hour."

"I'm not here to register," Sebastian said, amused by the way her lips turned down. "I'm a rider coach. I take it you're Cortes? I'm Daniels."

Her brows furrowed between her eyes, eyes he wished he could see. "Thomas never mentioned a fill in. My schedule says Davis not Daniels."

She walked past him, pulling out keys from her pocket, and slapped the clipboard to his chest as he came near. He watched her unlock the shed full of motorcycles. "I don't know. He called last night and asked me to fill in."

"Fine. I'll check with Thomas and see if Davis shows up. If not, I guess it's you. Ever teach before?"

"No." He tried not to get offended by her brisk manner.

She took the clipboard away from him. "You have your certification?"

"If you're asking if I took the course and passed the test, the answer is yes." His answer seemed to satisfy her.

"Fine, I'll need to see your license. We have ten riders today. We only take twelve, so there might be walk ins or no shows for the morning."

"Just tell me what you want me to do," he offered, keeping his eyes on her face. With an attitude like that, he bet most men probably only ever ogled her the first time they crossed her path.

"Once we have the course set up, I'll let you do the observing while I demonstrate the course. These are beginner riders and some of them need more instruction than others."

"As you wish," he said.

She glanced back at him. Unable to read her expression through her sunglasses, he wondered about the color of her eyes.

They worked together for the next half hour, starting up motorcycles, pulling them from the shed, and making sure they all had enough gas. She gave the orders and he obeyed, something he didn't mind for a change.

When the first rider came, Sebastian stood in front of the table and signed them in until each rider had been checked in. There was one no show and four unregistered riders show to fill in, but they had to send one away. A woman come with her boyfriend and would have to hang out the four hours for the morning session since they both came on one motorcycle.

The morning passed quickly, Cortes mounting her Yamaha and demonstrating the course, the other's following. At lunch, the group left, and they prepared for the next round. They'd both packed lunches. Sebastian's consisted of a half a sub and a bag of chips from last night's Subway run.

"I guess Davis isn't showing up," she said, sitting in the shaded patch of grass on the far end of the shed. It was a far cry cooler than the heating asphalt on an unusually hot June day.

"Guess you're stuck with me," he said, offering her a baked cheddar chip.

"You handled the guy with the Harley well. I admit, out of all of them, I figured he would be the one to drop his ride. There is always one, but this afternoon are the experienced riders. I should warn you, most of them are Ghosts, they come more for fun than for the learning aspect, and they like to give the new guy a hard time."

"Is that so? I think I can handle it. You said they're ghosts?"

"Ghost Riders." She drank from a thermos filled with what he suspected was water. "They're the local motorcycle gang around here. Their club house is on the more populated section of town. Since you ride, they may try to recruit you."

"No, thanks." Been there done that, but he wouldn't go there again .

"You sound like you know them pretty well." He wanted to get to know her better, but the alarms in his head flashing 'danger,' warned him to take a step back.

"That's because they consider me one of their own. Once

a Ghost Rider always a Ghost Rider," she said, but from the sound of her voice, there was more. A wistfulness or maybe more of a defeated reflection. She straddled her ride like she owned it. In his experience in clubs, most women had old men, boyfriends or husbands who claimed them. Another reason to keep his involvement with her professional.

"I ride alone," he said.

She pushed her sunglasses up in her hair, and for the first time that day, he caught the color of her eyes. Liquid amber, like the warm rays of sun peeking through a tall jar of sun tea on his mother's back porch.

Feeling a little too warm, Sebastian rose, cleaned up his lunch, and figured he had enough time to take a walk before the next session.

The law enforcer inside him scanned the area again, deciding he wouldn't go far, not wanting to leave her alone or unprotected. It had been months since he thought of his last assignment, the people he left, and the one he failed.

The old wound in his shoulder started to ache. The sooner he got this gig over with the sooner he could put distance between him and the attraction he found for the curvy, long-legged, rider coach.

By the afternoon session, Caitlyn shed her leathers and applied another coat of sunscreen across her nose and cheeks. She adjusted the bill of the ball cap to keep the sun from her face and walked out amongst the bad boys of the Ghost Riders who came to give her a hard time.

Her father, Welder, sent them, thinking to discourage her from instructing anymore. A woman's place was alongside her man, taking care of him, rearing a family. For many those notions sounded outdated and chauvinistic. Which was why

Caitlyn decided to show the members of the Ghost Riders she could hold her own, with or without a man.

Groover and Blue were the first to show. Silas supporters, they all still thought of her as Silas's old lady. The divorce, the fact he went to prison, neither made a difference. No man in a hundred miles radius would dare ask her out amongst the locals. She belonged to the Ghosts and her father approved of no one worthy of taking Silas's place.

"You'll need a helmet for the course," she told Blue. Bald beneath the blue and red Yankee's bandana, the large, muscled man grunted.

"No helmet. No ride on my course," she said.

"His head is hard as granite," Groover vouched for him.

"You know I don't wear a helmet," Blue said.

Caitlyn shrugged. "Not my rules. You want to take the course; you wear a helmet. I can look in the shed and see if I have a spare."

"And I'll crack it in half before my head ever splits," said Blue.

"That's the point," Caitlyn said, watching Blue's face turn from all-knowing to confusion.

"You telling me I can't participate in this sissy parade without a helmet?" Blue asked.

"Groover does," Caitlyn pointed out, spotting Daniels coming back from his walk. A nice enough guy, who seemed a little lost and overly willing to let her boss him around. Too bad as pushovers weren't really her thing, but not arguing at every instruction was nice.

"Groover has Jello for brains," Blue said.

"Then it's a good thing he wears a helmet," she said.

"Where is Davis? He'll put an end to this."

"He's not here. Now, I've got more people to sign in so we can start on time." She pointed a pen at him. "Helmet."

Blue swore. "No way."

"If the lady says you need a helmet, then you wear a helmet," Daniels stepped alongside her behind the table.

"Who are you?" Groover asked.

"New guy," Caitlyn said, a little surprised to see Daniels taking her side.

"The others are on their way," Blue said.

Instead of taking it as a threat, Daniels answered, "Good. Looking forward to meeting them."

Blue grumbled and he and Groover stepped aside for the next person. Due to half the class roster consisting of Ghost Riders, they had another full class. Blue had too many points against his license for him to risk walking away from the class. It was this or he would have to ride behind Groover to get to the next Ghost Rider meeting. An Image of the older man straddled behind Groover almost made her laugh out loud. She kept It In, although Daniels squinted at her and she averted her gaze. The last thing she needed was for the new guy to take It the wrong way. Afterall, she might have to work with him again in the future.

The rider coach program ran through the state. It was good money on the side during the riding season. Those wanting to get their license or needing to refresh on their skills filled the class. Then those, like Blue, came after meeting up with citations took the courses as mandated to keep their licenses.

Butch and his old lady, Zelda showed up, her hair flaming green, and it appeared she had gotten a new nose piercing. She rode on the back of his touring bike. She wouldn't be taking the class, but settled near the shed, laying out her jacket and going to business of filing down her nails. Somewhere in the pockets, Caitlyn guessed, the woman had brought everything she needed for both a mani and a pedi. Butch and Zelda were inseparable, especially since last year when Zelda got diagnosed with ovarian cancer. Not that most of the Ghost

Rider men were over-protective of their women in the first place.

Caitlyn noticed no women had signed up for the course this afternoon. Usually, Davis and she had an agreement. She did the demonstration and he stayed out of her way. Mainly, because the guy was lazy and looking for easy pay.

"Your turn." She turned toward Daniels, deciding to test her new partner. "Think you can handle showing these boys the ropes this time around?"

"I can do that. Which exercise are we with starting with?"

She pulled out the cards and showed him.

"I can do that." He headed toward his bike.

"Use one of the student bikes, less wear and tear on yours."

He looked between his bike and o ne of the student bikes. Students had a choice of riding their own or one provided for them. Most liked to ride their own. They were more comfortable handling it. She'd rode her own, but Daniels didn't remark on it. He headed for one of the student bikes.

Pity far from her mind as Daniels demonstrated the exercise and the members of the Ghost Riders decided to critique his riding as he finished.

Daniels took it in good humor, surprising her. Blue asked for a repeat performance, and Groover was the first to slip up and miss the turn around the third cone.

Impressed as she was by his handling skills, Caitlyn had more than herself to think about when it came to relationships with men. And of course, there was always guys like Groover, Blue, and her father, Welder, who failed to recognize she was a free woman.

SNEAK PEEK OF SEBASTIAN

"Have you thought about what you want to do?" Thomas Yeats asked him. "Maybe it's time you think about pledging again, settling down. You've got family here, right?"

He had family back in Johnstown, not the blood kind, but the members of the Thunder Valley Riders were his brothers and sisters. After all these years, it didn't feel right to pledge to another club. He swore he left motorcycle clubs and getting involved in that kind of business behind him. He took the rider coach job as a way to make some cash. His father would pull him into the family business, giving tours on horseback along with his sister. He had no right coming back to Gettysburg and invading his sister's life. He couldn't protect her back then, he couldn't protect Audra from pike. What would happen when his past caught up to him?

And it would.

"I'll take you up on the offer of the place to stay, but I'm not taking any pledges."

"Fair enough," Yeats shrugged off his leather jacket. "Soon or later, though, you should let your family know you're alive. How long has it been since you spoke to them?"

"I get photos and a text from Mom every once in a while.

She and my father took a cruise," he said, trying to remember the last time he got a text from them. It was before his last case went down the toilet and he switched phone numbers. He kept the old phone and kept it turned off in case anyone was tracking it. He hadn't told his parents about getting shot or having to leave Johnstown. Even at thirty-one, his mother would still worry for him.

Yeats scratched his chin. "Same will be upset if you don't tell her you're near."

"You've been watching out for her?"

Yeats shrugged. "She's dating some teacher that moved here last year. He comes to church with her on Sundays and I hear he helps her out at the stables when your parents are gone."

Sebastian went to the old teal colored fridge and pulled out a bottle of water. There wasn't much else inside beside a few take-out cartons of Chinese and a half gallon of milk. "You didn't have to do that."

"That's what friends are for," Yeats said.

Sebastian eased down in a chair at the kitchen table. His legs ached and his lower back. He knew Yeats from high school, and even back then Sebastian knew his friend had an eye for his sister. Sebastian warned, no threatened, Yeats to steer clear of his twin, but it had been Yeats who found her the night of prom after she'd been violated. And, it had been Yeats who talked him down from killing the jock who hurt his sister.

Sebastian guzzled down the water trying to flush out the memories of his past. Coming back here had been a bad idea, but he couldn't leave now. He promised Yeats he'd stay for the summer and took the rider coach job until he figured out his next move. Razek, his former boss, and chief of police in Johnstown, still held his badge and offered to help him relocate to another job on another police force.

He touched his shoulder, the ache more in his mind than physical.

"Your shoulder still bothering you?" Yeats turned a chair, took a seat and leaned against the back of it with his arms propped on top. "Maybe I shouldn't have talked Davis into switching sites and gave you more time to heal."

"It's not the shoulder."

Sebastian had a hole inside him, so big, so gaping, and painful he doubted it would ever heal. He stuffed it with regrets for the past four months. Crawling into that hole and hiding away, just like Razek wanted him to do and he said he wouldn't. Nothing would ever fill the huge, hollow emptiness, inside him. He wasn't a cop anymore, nor did he deserve to get involved in other people's lives. He could endanger them all.

Which is why if he should have never come here, should have changed his name, and should have accepted Razek's help. But he'd called Yeats, his old buddy from high school and hauled his butt north away from the Sharks and the haunting memories of the woman he couldn't save.

"Listen man, I figured this was a good fit for you, but if the job is too much then say the word."

"It's not the job."

Sebastian twisted up his empty water bottle. Spilling his guts to Yeats would get his old friend in trouble. Haden, his friend and club brother back in Johnstown knew too much and Sebastian hated cutting ties with him.

He couldn't get close to people. Not anymore, or they would get hurt. They'd be in danger. And, he fisted his hand around the crushed plastic, they might die.

"Caitlyn?"

Sebastian dropped the crumpled bottle on the table. "Cortes?"

Yeats grinned. "She called in to check on you."

Sebastian's chest tightened. "What did you tell her?"

"The truth." Yeats lifted a shoulder. "I told her Davis was useless and you were replacing him."

"That's it?" Sebastian asked.

Yeats smirked. "Don't fall for the good looks. Caitlyn's pretty, sure, but she's not worth taking a bullet to the head. You got by with a shoulder wound, but her old man Silas will go for the kill."

"She's married?" Sebastian got up, feeling he needed to pace. What was he doing asking about her anyway? She wasn't his business. The fact she had an old man should have come as a relief. The Ghosts had made it known she was one of them, and he didn't need to get involved. Not. Again.

"Divorced, but the Ghost don't believe in divorce. They're not the worse club in the county, but Welder holds his beliefs as law."

"Welder?"

"Cat's father."

"And you paired me to work with her?" Because the last thing he needed was another bounty on his head from another outlaw motorcycle club. Friend or no friend, Sebastian couldn't tell Yeats the whole truth. He left the force, and Yeats knew something happened to make him leave. He wouldn't talk about it, and Yeats didn't ask. It was better this way for both of them.

"Just stick to your plan man. You got nothing to worry about."

No women. No clubs. No getting involved with the law.

And stay away from family.

If he could do that, then Sebastian might have a chance at keeping his past at bay.

"Order up!"

Caitlyn shoved another large pizza with the works in the

box and moved on to the next order. The back door was propped open and the air conditioner in the side wall hummed, but neither kept the sweat from rolling down her forehead.

She took a moment to step outside, pull off her bandana to pat her face. Leaning back against the wall she took a deep breath, wishing for once she'd remember to grab a bottle of water when she stepped out.

The phone in her pocket rang. She pulled it out. The number blinking on the screen made her tilt her head. "Hello."

"Caitlyn Cortes?"

She pressed the bandana to the side of her face. "Who is this?"

"Main Street Pub."

"The one inside the hotel?"

"Yes."

Caitlyn stuffed the bandana into her mouth for a moment to silence the scream curling up her throat.

"Ms. Cortes?"

Removing the banana she said, "I'm on my way."

On the other end of the phone, the man paused, unsure what to say. She already knew what he would tell her. She sighed, as the guy said, "Okay," and hung up.

One hundred and twelve days, she thought, what a waste.

Stepping back into the hot kitchen she found the manager, Regina.

"I'm sorry. I'll be back as soon as I can."

Regina planted her hand on her hip. "We're short tonight without Leo. I need you to come back."

"I'm sorry," Caitlyn apologized again.

Regina said, "Just get there and get back."

Caitlyn worked for Regina's family off and on since she graduated high school. They knew the drill as well as she did. No one else would let her work part-time like this, not in a million years, but she grew up in this town, and pity always won people over.

Chucking her apron in the bin and grabbing her keys, she headed for the hotel.

Inside the hotel's pub, she took a moment for her eyes to adjust to the dim interior. There, at the bar, with old Terry and Lucas, sat her father. He slammed his glass on the bar, demanding service, while Terry chuckled and Lucas took a sip from a long neck bottle. Beside him an empty glass sat.

Why they chose the Gettysburg Hotel, was beyond her. Usually they went further out of town, found a dive or one of their regular hangouts where they drank and relived their old glory biker days. Why weren't they at the Ghost Riders' Tavern? Blue ran the place and kept spare rooms for club members who needed to sleep it off after club gatherings.

Welder could have walked to get here, and that made the most sense. One too many DUI's and her father lost his ability to legally drive. She'd taken the keys to his Roadster and hid them.

Not paying attention, she moved to go toward Welder, when someone stepped in front of her. They collided, and he grabbed her shoulders to steady her. Dirty blond hair and a scruff across his chin, Daniels murmured an apology.

The last thing she needed was to run into the rookie rider coach here.

Caitlyn's heart rattled in her chest. Not wanting to cause any more attention than Welder created with his buddies, she tried to play it cool. She smiled, but Daniels took one look at her with those sinfully blue eyes and cut through her toughest of defenses.

The softness of his gaze stilling the anxiety inside her for the moment.

"I'm fine," she said, hoping he'd let her go and they could both move on.

Daniels cleared his throat, dropping his hands from her shoulders. "You sure?"

Another outburst erupted from Welder at the bartender. "Fill'er up now!"

"If you'll excuse me," she tried to remain calm like she did when they were on the course. Only then, her drunk father hadn't been causing a scene.

Pulling up those invisible shields she'd gotten so good at constructing, Caitlyn wiped her hands down the side of her worn jeans. The entire place smelled of molten brew and smoke, and she wanted to get out of here pronto. She blink to keep her eyes from watering.

Daniels stepped out of her way, distracted by her father yelling at another man behind the bar, she couldn't look back at Daniels, and she wanted to, despite knowing it would bring her more trouble. Men were trouble. And she had enough troubles on her own.

"Papa," she said, staying back far enough out of his reach.

Welder swiveled around. His eyes glassy and his lips curling up in a sneer. "What are you doing here?"

Caitlyn licked her lips, careful to choose her next words. So far, they hadn't attracted any additional attention in the hotel's bar. She noticed Daniels staying nearby.

"I'm on break. I thought you'd like to go somewhere else. I can drive you."

Welder shook his head, his dark hair peppered with grey.

"If we wanted to leave I'd have taken him," Lucas spoke up. The older biker glared at her. His leather ties swinging under his arms.

"Go away. Go back to your job," Welder waved her away.

Her lips thinned as she pressed them together. She noticed the bartender taking several steps back.

"The night's young," Terry, her father's old friend, beat on his chest. "We're just getting started."

The bartender was young, barely old enough to serve

alcohol by the looks of him. The younger man's eyes widened and Caitlyn took a deep breath. Another man, one wearing a suit and a tie, came behind the bar.

"Why don't you all hang out at the house?" She could call Regina and see if she could bring Owen in to work with her for a few hours. "I'll grab some pies and it will be like old times."

"I'm staying here," Terry grumbled.

Lucas waved her off. She placed her hands on her hips, irritated by her father's friends coming to town and screwing up his sobriety.

"Why not the Ghost Riders' Tavern. I'm sure you haven't seen Blue yet," she said.

"Kicked us out," Welder snarled. "Wouldn't give me a drink!" He pointed to his chest, his cheeks turned ruddy.

"Well that explains it," she muttered, throwing up a silent thanks to God that Blue had enough honor to keep from giving her father a drink.

"Don't you got some place to be?" Terry narrowed his gaze on her.

"Yeah, I do." Caitlyn snapped back at him. "And I plan on getting there as soon as you all clear out from here."

"I'm staying here," Terry said.

"We've got rooms for the weekend. Taking your rider course tomorrow night and Saturday," Lucas said.

"You can take it when you return to Florida. They've got them down there, too," Caitlyn said, inching closer to Welder. "Come on Papa, you promised you'd watch out for Owen."

Welder snorted. "The kid's old enough to take care of himself. Now be off!" Welder waved his hand, knocking Caitlyn back. She met two hands again to steady her.

"Where's my drink?" Welder demanded.

She glanced back and found Daniels at her back. He shook his head, not at her, but the bartender who held up his hands.

"We're done serving you for the night," the man in the suit said.

"What? My suit not fancy enough for you? I told you boys we should have gone across town," Welder said. "Why we meeting here again?"

"We're staying here while in town," Terry said.

Fury radiated down her bones at her father's old riding buddies, they knew her father was working on staying sober. It was almost seven in the evening and her father was soused. She started her shift at three, having finished up the paperwork for the rider coach course registrations for the upcoming weekend. It gave her enough time to check on Owen and get ready for shift at the pizza place.

How long after she left for work had Terry and Lucas come calling at the house? Or had Welder called them? And on a Thursday. Caitlyn tried to draw in all her emotions, truck them away for later. She drew up her frame, standing tall near Daniels. His presence and unwelcome comfort.

"I'll drink if I want to drink!" Welder exclaimed.

And that's when the pub went quiet, and Caitlyn froze in place. Welder's death glare landed on her, the black of his pupils enraged. Inside her head she chanted she was not afraid, but Daniels must have felt the slight twitch for he stepped in front of her.

"You won't get it here," Daniels said.

The man in the suit stepped closer to the bar between them. "No more," he confirmed. "You have reached your limit at this establishment. You must leave, please."

"You heard the manager, Papa. Let's go. I have to get back to work and you left Owen alone."

ABOUT THE AUTHOR

Growing up on a farm in Pennsylvania, Susan Lower yearned for adventure. A woodsy gal, Susan prefers camping over going to the beach any day. Still a farm girl at heart, Susan writes fast action reads filled with cowboys, heroes, and hope. She writes both western historical and contemporary romances, romantic suspense, and has been itching to one day write a mystery or thriller. Christmas is her favorite holiday, and she loves to write resilient characters struggling to overcome the complications of life while holding their values and strengthening their faith.

To learn more about Susan's books, sign up for her bimonthly email that includes exclusive excerpts, giveaways, and other goodies. http://susanlower.com/newsletter-sign-up/

ACKNOWLEDGMENTS

I'm married to a rider coach—a member of the motorcycle safety community that teaches motorcyclists how to properly and safety ride their motorcycles. This series has been a long time coming.

In addition to being a rider coach, my husband and I are members of our local Christian Motorcycle Association chapter. A member asked me when I was going to write a sweet motorcycle series, and here it is. I'm sorry it took so long.

A special thanks goes out to all the rider coaches trying to keep our motorcyclists safe. Also, special thanks to the Glory Land Riders and the Sonrise Riders for their fellowship, support, and the outreaches they do for our local communities, in which my husband and I have been participants. For Charlie, to whom this book series is dedicated, and Bob and Steve for coming by the house and including our kids in club activities. Although, the summer ice cream runs remain my favorite, always.

Writing a book is more of a marathon than a sprint, and I couldn't hit the finish line without my accountability partner and proofreader, Linda Au; my editor, Celeste Jones; Averi

Hope, for the cover design; my Thursday writing ladies; and you, my dear reader.

This might not have been the book you were expecting, but I hope you stick around for the rest of the ride as Sebastian's story is next. He and Caitlyn are about to discover that trust and a little faith can lead down the right road.

Made in the USA
Monee, IL
23 June 2025

19860841R00125